PRAISE FOR THE NOVELS OF
ED GORMAN

"Highly entertaining." —*Los Angeles Times*

"A Western for grown-ups . . . written in a lean, hard-boiled style." —*Publishers Weekly*

"Ed Gorman writes like a dream even when he's recounting nightmares. His fiction grips, entertains, and resonates in memory long after you close his books." —Dean Koontz

"Sweetly nostalgic . . . the kind of hero any small town could take to its heart." —*The New York Times Book Review*

"A superb storyteller." —Paula Guran

"Gorman's style is just right—terse, sharp, not a superfluous word." —*Library Journal*

"Genuinely affecting." —*The Wall Street Journal*

"Joyously precise period detail . . . [a] shrewd, affectionate slice of Americana. The governor of Iowa should give veteran Gorman the key to the state." —*Kirkus Reviews*

"What a pleasant treat this book is!" —Carolyn See, *The Washington Post*

SHOOT FIRST

ED GORMAN

BERKLEY BOOKS, NEW YORK

THE BERKLEY PUBLISHING GROUP
Published by the Penguin Group
Penguin Group (USA) Inc.
375 Hudson Street, New York, New York 10014, USA
Penguin Group (Canada), 90 Eglinton Avenue East, Suite 700, Toronto, Ontario M4P 2Y3, Canada
(a division of Pearson Penguin Canada Inc.)
Penguin Books Ltd., 80 Strand, London WC2R 0RL, England
Penguin Group Ireland, 25 St. Stephen's Green, Dublin 2, Ireland (a division of Penguin Books Ltd.)
Penguin Group (Australia), 250 Camberwell Road, Camberwell, Victoria 3124, Australia
(a division of Pearson Australia Group Pty. Ltd.)
Penguin Books India Pvt. Ltd., 11 Community Centre, Panchsheel Park, New Delhi—110 017, India
Penguin Group (NZ), Cnr. Airborne and Rosedale Roads, Albany, Auckland 1310, New Zealand
(a division of Pearson New Zealand Ltd.)
Penguin Books (South Africa) (Pty.) Ltd., 24 Sturdee Avenue, Rosebank, Johannesburg 2196,
South Africa

Penguin Books Ltd., Registered Offices: 80 Strand, London WC2R 0RL, England

This is a work of fiction. Names, characters, places, and incidents either are the product of the author's imagination or are used fictitiously, and any resemblance to actual persons, living or dead, business establishments, events, or locales is entirely coincidental.

SHOOT FIRST

A Berkley Book / published by arrangement with the author

PRINTING HISTORY
Berkley edition / January 2006

Copyright © 2006 by Ed Gorman.

ISBN: 0-425-20821-4

BERKLEY®
Berkley Books are published by The Berkley Publishing Group,
a division of Penguin Group (USA) Inc.,
375 Hudson Street, New York, New York 10014.
BERKLEY is a registered trademark of Penguin Group (USA) Inc.
The "B" design is a trademark belonging to Penguin Group (USA) Inc.

PRINTED IN THE UNITED STATES OF AMERICA

10 9 8 7 6 5 4 3 2 1

TEN YEARS AGO

*O*N THE TRAIN *back home, the four men spoke
very little.*

*On the journey out, they'd been loud and drunk, the
two of them who were handsome even flirting a bit with
married women whose husbands had stepped out of the
bar car for a while. They were wealthy, and let everybody know it; and if they weren't powerful in this state
adjoining their own, they certainly dropped the right political names to be taken seriously by other successful
men.*

*The colored waiter named Seth remembered them be-
cause they had tipped so freely. With what he'd made on
them, he was able to buy his three children some used
shoes to make the trip to the colored schoolhouse that
had opened recently.*

He wondered what had happened to them during

their week-long vacation. Because now they were not only quiet, they were sullen, and quick to anger. Two of them got in a fistfight right in the bar car. It was no fun separating them, either. They were sturdy men in their forties and knew how to throw punches.

There was no flirting, no noisy toasts, and a minimum of tipping. Before, they'd spent a good deal of the time sleeping and eating, fortifying themselves for the amount of bourbon they were consuming. Drunks always told Seth that. You slept enough, you ate enough, you could consume all you wanted and never damage your liver. Seth was not an educated man, but he'd learned long ago that just because a white man sounded right didn't mean he was right.

Two of them sat at the ends of the bar, drinking that way. The other two sat at different small tables by the windows, staring out at autumn colors. Day and night they sat there on the two-and-a-half-day trip back home. The funny thing was, they never seemed to get drunk. They probably drank more per man than they had on the trip out, but they didn't seem drunk at all.

Yessir, something had happened to these men—something they'd done or had done to them—something terrible that had changed them. And just like that little child's story about Humpty Dumpty, Seth doubted that you'd ever be able to put them back together again. Not the way they'd been on the trip out, anyway.

On the last night, just before Seth reached the end of this particular trip, one of the other waiters nudged him as they passed in the narrow corridor of the roaring train. With a nod, he directed Seth's attention to a par-

ticular door. Seth had delivered both food and drink here several times. It belonged to one of the four men.

Seth put his ear to the door and what he heard shocked him. Now Seth wasn't shocked easily. On trains he had seen sex of every kind, including a couple of men kissing. He had seen gambling where small fortunes were lost. And he had seen a man plunge a knife into the throat of another after learning that the now-dead man had seduced the killer's wife. What could possibly shock him in this year of 1878?

Weeping was what shocked him. A grown man weeping with the unembarrassed abandon of a child.

The other waiter grinned and nudged Seth in the ribs. But Seth didn't smile because he knew that this man was weeping over whatever they had done—or had done to them—on their vacation.

Seth saw nothing amusing about this, even if it had happened to an arrogant white man who'd once stomped around as if God had done signed over the entire planet to him.

No, sir. Even for a man you might hate, this kind of weeping was nothing to feel good about. Nothing to feel good about at all.

PART ONE

ONE

IT WAS HOT under the black slicker and matching rain hat. Bitter scalding late-summer rain. Slanting down so hard it sounded like gunfire every time it touched anything metal. And a ground fog that only made the night darker and more difficult to move around in.

Reed Matthews knew exactly where he was going on this night of September 8, 1888, in the town of Butte City, Colorado. His night deputy had sent a runner saying that there had been shots heard at the home of Gerald Soames, one of the three richest men in the valley, a man who'd lived in a tent for six years until his gold strike came in fifteen years ago. Now he lived in a Victorian-style mansion on the northern edge of town where all the rich men had their estates.

Matthews walked rather than rode. The job of sheriff in a town of ten thousand was pretty much sedentary these days. His puffy belly testified to that fact. He walked now whenever he could. He had faith in Harold Lincoln, the deputy already on the scene. Harold could take care of things until Matthews showed up.

Lightning and thunder always made him feel like a boy again, at the mercy of vast cosmic forces far scarier than the boogeyman his boyhood friends liked to talk about. Tonight was no exception. He winced every time thunder lashed the sky. The sight of lightning stunned him for a moment with its profane beauty—but then he always remembered what it preceded.

Not much traffic tonight, couple wagons, couple horses, all the passengers lost inside their own slickers. One of them was Doc McGinty. Every time his own job started ruining his mood and depriving him of sleep, all Matthews had to think of was Doc McGinty. Now there was one rough tough job.

McGinty shouted for Matthews to hop on the wagon, but Matthews waved him past.

The leaded windows of the Victorian home gleamed with lamplight. A small crowd, most in slickers, had gathered around the narrow front porch. The mortuary wagon was already there. This would be a profitable job for that tightwad Timothy G. Bevens. Soames would receive a funeral that would rile the pharaohs of ancient Egypt with envy.

From somewhere within the house, raw relentless sobbing overrode all other sounds. That would be Widower Soames's unmarried daughter Martha. Matthews knew her slightly—Matthews being an eligible bachelor, Soames had invited him out here a few times for dinner and a not-incidental couple hours in front of the fire-place with Martha.

He stepped inside the lavish home that just barely averted being an overdecorated joke. The Victorian style called for the kind of ornamentation that could be dupli-cated in glass, wood, metal, and paper. By comparison, the exterior gingerbreading was understated. Matthews figured when he made his first hundred thousand or so (ha-ha), he'd buy a big fancy house but then keep it rel-atively empty. Walking around echoing rooms would give him a real thrill.

Harold Lincoln walked up. "Shot. C'mon, I'll show you."

Martha was on the second floor. Apparently, some-body had closed her door because her sobbing was muted now.

The den was as Matthews remembered it. Persian rugs, three floor-to-ceiling bookcases, a huge stone fire-place, a desk half the size of a skating pond, and a bar stocked with liqueurs and other alcoholic imbibements that came from as far away as Iceland.

Soames, a portly man in his fifties with a Vandyke beard, was slumped in his tall leather chair behind his desk. He wore what he frequently wore, a brocaded vest—this one red—a white shirt, a dark ascot, and sleeve garters that matched the vest. One of the local jokes was that old Soames looked like the barkeep in the world's most successful whorehouse. His manner of dress didn't match the style of his house at all, as daugh-ter Martha frequently reminded him.

The bullet hole was right in the center of his forehead.

It hadn't bled much. The ruffled white shirt had been spared.

The closer Matthews got, the stronger the odors of feces and blood became. There was also the indefinable but uniform stink of death.

"You talk to anybody?" he asked Harold.

"The butler. He and the maid were playing euchre in the kitchen. He heard the shot."

"Just one?"

"That's what he said."

"Where was Martha?"

"In her room. She said she'd only talk to you."

Matthews walked the perimeter of the den. He looked for anything in the way of remarkable footprints. They'd likely be wet, the killer's. The trouble was, a number of people had obviously tramped through here already.

"Harold, go and ask the butler and the maid how many people had a key to the house."

"Already did. They did and the old man and the daughter. Nobody else."

"There's a side porch. Somebody might've gotten in that way."

"I checked that out, too. Locked from the inside."

Matthews smiled. "You've been reading those magazines I gave you."

"Every chance I get."

Matthews subscribed to several magazines for peace officers. Most of the articles were about "scientific detection" as it was developing in London and Paris, especially. A lot of interesting things were being done.

They spent the next twenty minutes checking every

room in the house but the one Martha was still weeping in. According to the magazine articles, they should look for "clues" that might be as small as a single button nobody could account for.

At one point, Matthews went to a window on the second floor that looked over the front yard. The mayor's buggy was just pulling up. The crowd numbered at least a hundred now. This was the sort of event people enjoyed, whether they'd admit it or not. It was natural for people to be interested in the lives of the rich, especially when those lives included murder. This was just as good as a storybook — hell, much better. The dead man was somebody they'd actually known. Who could ask for a better story than that?

He pulled his pocket watch from his slicker and said, "She's been quiet for ten minutes. Now's probably a good time to go up and talk to her."

He knocked, waited.

She opened the door, a rangy woman with a pretty if angular face, one now deeply reddened from crying. She wore a long and elegant royal-blue dressing gown. Her left hand carried a drink of what appeared to be bourbon.

"Don't worry, Reed," she said. "I'm all cried out. I know how much you men hate crying."

The large, high-ceilinged room was as much a miniature den as it was a bedroom. While a canopied bed filled the eastern corner, an artist's easel and a half-painted canvas stood near the window. A small table held a variety of paints and brushes. Several canvases were stacked against the wall. The northern wall was taken up with a bookcase and a desk. Nearby was a corner with an elegant chair upon which rested a violin. A music stand sat in front of the chair.

"I spend quite a bit of time in my room," she said, obviously noticing how carefully he examined the place.

"Looks like it."

"I've always wanted one thing that was mine. Absolutely mine. That neither my father nor my mother had anything to do with. And this is it."

A hint of bitterness in her voice surprised him. Yes, the room was all hers. But it was their money that had made it possible.

"Some whiskey, Reed?"

"I wouldn't pour it out."

She fixed him a drink from a small, impromptu sort of bar and brought it back to him. She pointed to a couch. "Why don't we sit down?" Once they were seated, she said, "I've been drinking a lot."

He'd heard that from a number of people in town. Service people, mostly, who worked on the estate in various ways. A few reports had her drunk as early as ten A.M.

"Maybe you'd better back off a little, Martha."

She said, as if she hadn't heard him, "And tonight at dinner I threw my whiskey in Father's face."

He could see how drunk she was. She wasn't at the point of weaving or slurring her words badly. But she was close. "Any particular reason you wanted to tell me those things?"

"Because that sonofabitch Tyrell'll tell you if I don't."

Tyrell—Matthews never had heard the man's first name—was the imperious butler.

"He doesn't like me," she said.

"Butlers can always be fired."

"Yes, and he damned well will be, too, you can bet on that."

He sipped his sour mash and let the silence speak for him. He wanted to make her nervous enough to keep saying things she shouldn't without first consulting a lawyer. He was sitting next to a vastly unhappy, maybe even insane woman. He could almost feel the way anxiety and pain and despair radiated from her.

He said, "Any particular reason you threw a drink in your father's face tonight?"

She shrugged. "He chased off Mike Wooden."

"I guess I don't know who that is."

"Was. He's dead now. He was the love of my life, Reed. I was twenty years old and I wanted to marry him. This was long before your time in town here. I wanted to marry him. I was pregnant." She angled her face so he could see her expression clearly. A cold smile bloomed like a winter flower. "The icy old maid everybody snickers about and pities in town? Well, she got knocked up by a common laborer. My father made me go to a special doctor in Denver and then I wasn't pregnant anymore. My father was always tidying things up in his life. He tidied my pregnancy up real well. I got an infection from the doctor he sent me to. I nearly died. But I suppose my father figured it was better to die without carrying a baby out of wedlock than to live with a bastard in my belly."

"What happened to this Mike Wooden?"

"He just disappeared."

"You never heard from him again?"

She shrugged. "It seems so long ago." For the first time, her words were slurred. She said: "My father either threatened him away or bribed him away. Or killed him. I could never figure out which."

"You really think your father would have him killed?"

"Not 'have him killed,' Reed. He hated the idea that this man had laid his hands on me so much, I don't doubt my father killed him personally. He was a very strong man, my papa."

Matthews said, "Did you kill your father, Martha?"

She smirked. "I knew we'd get around to that sooner or later."

"You didn't answer my question."

"I need another drink."

"You still didn't answer my question."

She laughed. "God, so many times I wanted to kill him. He was insufferable. He really was. You know something, Reed?"

"What's that?"

"I don't think he ever doubted a decision in his life. Think about that. An entire life lived without doubting yourself. Or having any regrets, either. I never once heard that man say he was sorry about anything. He never apologized to anybody for anything."

He took her wrist gently. "Martha. Listen to me. If you killed him, I'll help you. I promise. I'll make sure that everything goes as easy for you as possible. And I'm sure a local jury'd give you a fair hearing."

"That'd make it pretty easy for you, wouldn't it, Reed?"

"What would?"

"If I just confessed right now. Made your work so easy for you."

"I just want the truth is all, Martha. Right now I'm not worried about how easy or hard my work is. I just want the truth."

"Well," she said, "I didn't kill him. I wish I had but I didn't."

She was going to say something more but she didn't get the chance. Because just then she began vomiting all over herself, the hot mix of food, booze, and stomach juices splashing all over her elegant dressing gown.

TWO

FOR A LONG time, his rain-soaked clothes had bothered him. He'd imagined his throat was starting to get scratchy. He'd also barked the palms of his hands and his kneecaps climbing the oak tree that sprawled to the west of the Soames mansion.

Once he reached the top of the tree, he forgot all about the cold, the soaking unrelenting rain, the throat that really was getting scratchy.

All these minor nuisances got lost in the excitement of watching the crowd grow in front of the Victorian house. The crowd was the same way. It seemed to have forgotten all about the stabbing, unceasing rain, too.

He watched as the mortuary wagon wound slowly up the sweeping road. Watched as the cocky young newspaper reporter stumbled and fell on the front porch, to the great amusement of the onlookers. And watched as

Sheriff Reed Matthews came walking up the road to reach the estate grounds.

He wondered which would be worse for Matthews: to have a glimmer of an idea but not be able to do anything about it, or to be completely baffled by Soames's murder and have to keep stumbling — just as the reporter had stumbled — over a series of wrong answers, false leads, and dead ends?

Buggies, wagons, surreys. You'd think this was a holiday, the way vehicles kept coming. The way the crowd kept swelling.

In one of the second-floor windows, he could see Martha pacing back and forth. She was talking to somebody. Probably Sheriff Matthews.

Martha would never be able to carry on for her father. The old man had built or bought sawmills all over the West. He understood one thing above all where timber was concerned. To not only survive but prosper you had to stay current with the new developments, especially saws and the process of sawing timber. In the days of hand-sawing, manpower was all you had. But then waterpower came in to drive the saws and efficiency tripled. Back East this spring the old man had seen a demonstration of something unthinkable — a circular saw that went through timber in seconds.

Not that the old man would have shared any of this with Martha, whom he saw as hopelessly weak. He wondered if the old man had given her even a hint of what had happened and why his once-blessed life had turned cursed. He wondered if she'd found the letter Soames would have received a week ago.

Such a beautiful means of intimidation, a simple letter, written in such a way that only a handful of people on the entire planet could possibly know what it meant. Written in such a way that mere words would have had the effect of a knife blade on Soames.

He leaned back against a thick branch. The mortuary man and his helper were just now bringing Soames out on a stretcher. Covered, of course, so that the crowd would be denied the ultimate thrill, actually seeing the rich and resented man dead.

He was loaded on the wagon. The mortuary man and his helper then climbed up on the seat. The lone horse was reined into action. The wagon pulled slowly away, past the crowd that stood on tiptoe for a look at the body laid out in the wagon bed. Some of the women were crying. It was the proper thing to do, what they'd been trained to do. Inside, they probably wanted to smirk or laugh, as their husbands were doing now.

He situated himself so that he could stare straight down into the wagon bed when the vehicle passed below him. Soames would have hated all the people being on his lawn; hated being transported in a wagon as common and unadorned as this one. Most of all, he would have hated being murdered by somebody as uncouth as the killer.

He wondered what Sheriff Matthews was doing right now. . . .

"You mentioned a letter."

"Yes."

"You brought it to him personally?"

"Yes."

"Did you happen to read the return address?"

"The master's business is his own. I don't pry. I served two members of the royal family when they were here in the colonies for a time. You're not given that kind of honor if you pry."

My God, Matthews thought, here we had a bloody revolutionary war to rid ourselves of the Brits, and more than a hundred years later we're still imitating the worst of them.

Tyrell—his name was probably Ernie and he was probably from some clodhopper little town around here—the imperious Tyrell of the ridiculous cutaway coat and white tie said, "He was upset."

"After he read the letter?"

"Yes."

He'd made a point of not calling Matthews "sir."

"How do you know he was upset?"

"He smashed an imported wine decanter against the wall."

"You saw him do it?"

"No, but I heard him. And of course, I had to pick up the pieces." For the first and only time, he sounded somewhat resentful of his station in life.

"It couldn't have just fallen?"

"Not hardly. It was clear across the room. Where he'd hurled it."

"Any other way you could tell he was upset?"

Now, for the first and only time, Matthews got the impression that Tyrell lied.

"No."

"You're sure?"

"Yes."

"You sound like you're holding something back."

"I can't help how I sound."

They sat at the kitchen table. Harold came in. "You want to take a look at something?"

"Now?"

"I think you'd better."

Matthews looked at Tyrell. "Nothing else to tell me? You're sure about that?"

"Quite sure."

Matthews sighed. "I'll want to talk to you again. Probably tomorrow."

All Tyrell did was nod.

Matthews followed Harold out the back entrance of the mansion. He pulled on his slicker and hat as they walked. He didn't look forward to getting battered by the rain again.

"What's going on?" Matthews said when they were outdoors and nobody could eavesdrop on them.

"The barn over there?" Harold said.

"Yeah. What about it?"

"I think we got something. Surprised the shit out of me."

"So it'll surprise the shit out of me, too?"

"I'm pretty sure it will."

"I get a hint, Harold, or you going to keep me guessing?"

Harold stopped. The rain smashed and crashed against their slickers. "What if I told you we found a fella sleeping off a drunk in there?"

"I'd say that sounds promising."

"And what if I also told you that the maid told me that this fella is a former worker for Soames who threatened to kill him this afternoon?"

"I don't suppose he has a gun on him that was recently fired, does he?"

Harold grinned. He had bad brown teeth. But right now Matthews didn't care if he had the worst teeth in the world. "That's exactly what he's got. A Colt that's been fired in the last couple hours."

THREE

H IS NAME WAS Soames, Ab for Abner Soames, and
he had been born to the river, specifically the Colorado River and the days of the great steamboats. He'd
had a damned good job at a mill when he was fourteen,
but he gave it up once he saw his first steamboat.

Ab rode the river. First as a lowly hand who had to
sleep right next to the coloreds, but eventually he'd become an expert at hauling a steamboat off one of the
many sandbars along the vast river. He had the knack.
He didn't know where the knack had come from, he
didn't even know how long it would last. But among
captains on the river he was legendary. The freckle-faced
Ab Soames who knew just what to do when you ran
aground in any fashion. He practiced "crawfishing" and
"grasshoppering," the two most common ways of
wrenching your vessel back into the stream. But he prac-

ticed them with a skill that bordered on the supernatural, or so it was said when the night was calm and the crew had turned to wine and telling tall tales of the Colorado.

Captains requested him, but the waiting line was long. By age twenty-five, he was able to afford his own fancy apartment and to fall in love with a fancy, educated woman.

Then came the night of the worst storm he'd ever encountered. Not even his knack could save the steamboat that night. It splintered and broke up on a ragged jut of rock that had somehow been overlooked when the navigational maps had been drawn up.

He was drunk when this happened. He awoke to a nightmare of cries and screams and a boat quickly being drowned in violently churning waters. He ran up to the deck only to see people pitching themselves over the side. A fire had started in the boilers. The passengers had obviously decided to take their chances with water rather than fire.

He was so drunk that the only thing he could think of was himself. He ran to the edge of the deck and was about to throw himself into the vortex of muddy water climbing the side of the ship when he heard the screams directly behind him.

A woman and her child had been smashed to the deck by a lashing wave. She was trying to regain her footing. With one hand, she clutched her baby. With the other she reached out in entreaty, like one of those poorhouse posters you saw where the ragged mother of six held her empty hands out begging you for a donation to the Salvation Army.

The water soaked him, the water blinded him. He could feel, despite the water, the fire that was roaring across the deck. It was the kind of heat that has no equivalent—a thousand desert suns focused on you all at the same time.

He pulled back from jumping. He'd been going to jump but he couldn't. He had to help the mother and her child.

Then the southern half of the deck was turned into a fireball as the second explosion erupted in a fireworks display that had an ugly beauty played off against the lonesome starry Western sky. He'd never known the screams of the dying could be so piercing; or that the cries of children could sadden him so inconsolably.

And yet in that moment—a moment was all he had; heroism is often defined by a single moment—in that moment, seeing how quickly the fireball was rolling up the deck, he looked at the mother and child who were so close and yet so far—

—looked at them and hurled himself over the side of the steamboat.

And yet he took them with him, of course, that poor mother and child. Because he was forevermore a man stalked by ghosts—their ghosts. No matter how much he drank, how much he gambled, how much he whored, how much he was compensated for wrenching steamboats off sandbars . . . no matter how fast or far he fled, they were with him.

The eyes of the woman, the cries of the little girl . . .

It wasn't long before he lost his so-called instinct. It wasn't long before he was as much a drunken hindrance as a help to any captain he worked for. It wasn't long before those who'd once halfway believed he was some sort of river wizard saw him as a ridiculous, overpaid, overpampered drunk.

If you asked him straight out about the years between being fired from the fourth and last of his steamboat lines and the hard sober day when he became the groundsman for the Soames mansion . . . he wouldn't have been much help. The rotgut had turned memory into vapors.

Then one day in a Louisiana town where the ghosts of the dead woman and her daughter were particularly chill . . . he had a vision that was almost religious in its oddness and intensity.

There stood his cousin Doria in a cowled robe telling him that his uncle Gerald Soames was going to take him in and sober him up and let him live on the mansion grounds in return for work, churchgoing, and an absolutely "dry" existence.

Four months later, after a prolonged stay in a hospital for drunkards, he appeared on the vast green dream of a lawn that surrounded his uncle's Victorian mansion. And became the groundsman.

Now, three years later, he opened one eye and watched Sheriff Reed Matthews approach him.

Matthews looked around the small room located in a corner of the barn. It was clean and orderly, single bed, comfortable reading chair, bureau, piece of strung rope to hang clothes, and a packing crate stacked with magazines and books.

Ab Soames lay on the floor rather than the bed. He had the look and stench of a frequent drunk, but Matthews had been assured that this was his only bender in all the time he'd been here. Three days it had lasted in town; on the fourth day they'd deposited him at the front gate of the mansion. He'd slept that one off, crept into the house in the middle of the night, stole a few more bottles of whiskey, and continued his bender.

Matthews said, "You grab an arm and I'll grab an arm."

Harold and Matthews yanked the man to his feet, dragged him to the chair, dropped him in it.

Matthews went over to the bureau, filled the wash pan, carried it back, and emptied all the water on the face and shoulders of Ab Soames.

The man cursed, sputtered, spluttered. Then cursed some more.

Matthews held up the Colt. "I believe this is your gun."

"I got drunk. I shouldn't have. I was good all those years. And then I—"

"Is this your Colt?" Matthews repeated patiently.

Soames sat up. He needed a shave and a bath badly. His white Sunday shirt and his black Sunday trousers crawled with grime of every kind. A man drinks all night long in a saloon—a man with no home nearby—he's liable to do some time on his hands and knees and sleeping in alleys.

Soames squinted. "There a big piece missing out of the right handle?"

"Yeah."

"Then it's mine."

"You kill your uncle?"

Soames sat back in his chair. He gave them a little dramatic presentation. First he wiped his face of water with great intensity; then he shook his head as if he were trying to knock a thought clean out of his mind; and finally he raised his suffering face up to Matthews. "My uncle's dead?"

"Uh-huh."

"Martha kill him?"

"I guess we had somebody else in mind."

"That why you're holdin' my Colt up?"

"Yeah. We're pretty sure the bullet came from your gun."

"I was too drunk to shoot anybody."

"It doesn't take a whole lot of effort, Mr. Soames."

Soames offered a half smile. " 'Mr. Soames.' Now I know you think I killed him." The smile didn't quite fit his face. "You saw where I was. On the floor. That's where I've been all the time since they brought me home. And the only reason I remember them bringin' me home was because Tyrell told me."

"I'm told you had an argument with your uncle."

"Shit, we had arguments all the time."

"What about?"

"Me not goin' into town, that's what. Three years I lived here and never once went into town. That's no life."

"How could he stop you?"

"He couldn't stop me goin' but he could stop me comin' back."

"Was that what you were arguing about earlier?"

"I guess."

"You don't remember?"

"Not exactly. But that was usually the problem."
Then: "No."

"'No' what?"

"No, that wasn't it. What we were arguing about."

"It's coming back to you."

"A little bit. He was firing me. That was it."

"For going on your bender?"

"Yeah. He was giving me twenty-four hours to clear out. He said he'd give me five hundred dollars in cash and then he never wanted to see me again. He said he didn't owe me or my mother anything else."

"You remember what you did then?"

Ab shrugged. "Probably shouted." He leaned forward and put his face in his hands. "I didn't hate him, you know."

"You sure argued a lot."

"There's a difference between hating somebody and arguing with them. I just wanted to get into town and stretch my legs a little. But he was right."

"How so?"

"The one and only time I finally did sneak off and head into town, look what happened. Could walk past a saloon without goin' in. I can remember that real clear. I kept walkin' up and down the street and listenin' to the music and smellin' the beer. Just walkin' back and forth. Couple of the old-timers on the porch kept laughin' at me. They knew what I was goin' through. I finally just walked right straight out of town. Didn't even stop to get my horse because I'd reined it too close to a saloon. Just walked right straight out of town on the stage road. I must've gotten a mile out of town. I felt pretty good about it. That I hadn't gone into a saloon, after all. But then at some point I just turned around and walked straight back to town and straight into a saloon. And that was that. I threw my whole life away."

He took his face from his hands and sat back in the chair. "I'm pretty sure I didn't kill him."

"A minute ago you were absolutely sure you didn't kill him."

"You know how it is when you're liquored up. But whether I think I did or I think I didn't, you're gonna arrest me anyway, right?"

"Right."

"I'd remember it if I killed him." Then: "I just remembered something."

"Yeah? What?"

"As I was walking toward my uncle's den—I saw somebody running out but I wasn't paying much attention so I didn't get a real look at him. Plus I was real drunk." Then: "I guess I must've gone in to see my uncle after they brought me back from town, too. Because it was night. I remember now. It had to be night because I can see my uncle leaning over to light his cigar off a lamp. It had to be night."

"You know something, Mr. Soames?"

"What?"

"You need to get real sober before we talk anymore. You keep contradicting yourself."

"I didn't hate him."

"But you were mad at him."

"But I didn't hate him."

Harold went over and got him on his feet. He cuffed him in front. Led him from the room and out to one rain-blasting night.

Matthews spent fifteen minutes checking the room. The place was one step up from a rented sleeping room. It felt of that particular kind of male loneliness. Isolated men, the days on their calendars left blank, unmarked by the events of family.

He was hot inside his slicker when he got outside again. The crowd had mostly dispersed. Harold and Soames waited under the overhang of the front porch. The wagon Martha had loaned them sat at the bottom of the steps, ready to go.

Matthews tied Harold's horse to the back of it. Harold led Soames to the wagon. Matthews rode on into town with them.

FOUR

AFTER SOAMES WAS in his cell, and after all the curious citizens had been cleared out of the office, Matthews turned everything over to Harold and started his walk home. The rain had finally slacked off. The air smelled pure and cold. He was tired, but then remembered that he needed to pick up candles. Annie Reynolds made them for most people, half her cottage work space, the other half her living quarters.

A light gleamed in the front window. He went up to the door and knocked.

She answered the door in a pair of butternuts and a yellow blouse, her dark hair combed out so that it reached her shoulders. Part of her prettiness was the imp lurking in the dark eyes and occasionally touching the small mouth. She had the kind of facial bones that would keep her looking young for a long time to come, that kind of kid-sister face that holds up for decades. She was little more than five feet tall and little more than ninety pounds.

She had a cup of coffee in her hand.

"Smells good," he said.

The furniture was spare and ran to what was called spool-turned Victorian, heavy and dark black walnut chairs and tables that she'd inherited from the previous renter, who'd had to leave town before his employer lodged a formal charge of embezzlement against him. There was an impersonality to the place that surprised Matthews. You'd expect something of her—she was such a strong personality—to be reflected in the place. But there wasn't so much as a photograph from her past.

As she bustled about, he told her what had happened tonight.

When they were seated in chairs by the fireplace, she said, "Bet there are a lot of sad people in town tonight."

"I'm not sure about that. Old Man Soames wasn't exactly beloved."

The imp grin. "That's what I meant. People are sad because they weren't the ones who got to kill him."

"What's that old saw about not speaking ill of the dead?"

She shook her head. "I never did understand that one, Reed. Hell, if you were a bad man in life, why should people get all teary-eyed about you when you die? We all have to die. There's nothing special in that."

He smiled. "Maybe they'll ask you to deliver the eulogy."

"I'd be happy to." The grin. "I'd deliver a eulogy that this town would never forget."

Matthews didn't know much about Annie except that she'd grown up in the slums of Chicago and come west here about six years ago. She was engaged twice but broke both commitments. Both spurned men said the same thing. She couldn't get over the bitterness she'd picked up in the slums. Her anger was said to terrify people. Matthews had never seen it personally. But he'd heard enough about her to stay away from her in any romantic way. Anyway, he had plenty of romance problems as it was. He had his own woman who wouldn't marry him. Karen Davies was her name.

He was in a comfortable rocking chair. He put his head back. Closed his eyes. "I guess we got our man."

"He didn't confess?"

"I don't think he really knows, he was so drunk and all."

"He's an odd one, Reed."

Matthews opened his eyes, raised his head off the back of the rocking chair. "If we started hanging 'odd ones,' there wouldn't be anybody left after a while."

"I'd be left."

He laughed. "You and I would be among the first that got hanged. We're not married, we don't have families, we don't own property, we don't go to church very often, we don't belong to any civic organizations."

She grinned. "You make us sound downright awful."

"In a way, we are. We aren't in the mainstream of our town. And people don't like that. If anything happens— like to Ab Soames—they turn on you. By eight o'clock tomorrow morning, this whole town will have him convicted and ready to hang."

"You arrested him. You must think you've got a pretty good case."

"I do. And I don't." He put his head back against the chair, closed his eyes again. The sounds of the fire popping, the waves of warmth burnishing him, the easy motion of the rocking chair . . . he wanted to put the whole thing out of his mind. "You know what it is."

"What what is?"

"He's not going to confess. I'll have to prove he did it. There're enough things against him now that a jury'll convict him and probably without much hesitation."

He finished his coffee and stood up. "I'd better get going. I'll have to get up real early tomorrow. It'll be a big day."

At the door, she handed him a dozen candles she had wrapped in newspaper. He took out the exact change and paid her with it. "Thanks for the coffee."

Then he was outside again.

The man sat on the edge of his bed in the darkened hotel room. He was still cold from having been in the tree so long tonight. He'd thought of taking a scalding hot bath but decided it was too much trouble. He simply came to his room and dried off. He sat here now staring at the list in front of him. The back of an envelope, nothing fancy. Pencil-scrawled list of names. Two of them had been checked off. Gerald Soames was now checked off. He'd done that earlier.

The sadness came upon him then, the kind of paralysis that gripped him following the murders of the men whose names appeared at the top of the list. Such a strange reaction, given his role in all this. It was a little like sex, he reasoned. Sex was a pleasurable thing, to be sure. And he partook every chance he got. But sometimes he was sad after sex. And he never knew why. He sensed it, too, in the women he was with. Sometimes, they were melancholy, too, afterward. It was all such a mysterious business, living, and sometimes it made no sense at all.

He rolled himself a smoke and took a deep drink from his pint of rye.

He tried not to think about Chicago and what it had been like there, seeing his little sister puke up blood because the water was bad in the slums. Pounding and pounding and pounding on the back of the man who was killing his mother even as he was screwing her, strangling her, killing her before the boy could finally stop him — stopping him finally by taking the butcher knife his older sister handed him and digging it deep into the back of the man's head. But it was too late anyway. Mom was dead. She always said that she was scared of half the men she slept with, what with so many prostitutes being murdered in Chicago that spring, a regular epidemic it was. And then his own little sister turning out the same way —

After he killed his mother's murderer, they put him in a hospital. For insane people, they said. They said that he really hadn't killed that man at all. That he'd only imagined that he had. That he, in fact, did that all the time. Imagined that he'd done certain things when he hadn't done them at all. His mother, they said, got drunk one night and fell in front of a trolley car. But he knew

they were lying to him. Knew that he'd killed that
man . . .

The hotel room smelled of dust, tobacco, sweated
mattress. He sat there in his robe, shivering slightly.

After a time, he raised the list up to the faint light
from the street lamp outside the window. It was time to
be thinking of the next name on the list.

FIVE

T HE FOLLOWING MORNING was typical of Matthews's days in law enforcement: a renegade rider, that being a ranch hand who rode to other ranches to collect straying horses, had been accused of ransacking part of a barn after the ranch owner argued with him about the "stray" horse in question; a mail-order cowboy, a lanky youth from Illinois out to write some newspaper stories about "the real West," had been slightly beaten and more than slightly robbed around dawn this morning; and two men wanted a peace officer to settle an argument about who owed what to whom where a six-shooter, or as they called it, a "hawg-leg," was concerned. Matthews wouldn't have gotten involved in any of this if his two deputies hadn't been at the courthouse giving depositions in two different cases.

The inquest for Gerald Soames was scheduled for

three P.M. There was no place in town to escape talk and speculation about the matter. Matthews had to leave the office three times before the inquest, and each time he got surrounded by folks who wanted to talk about the Soames murder.

Ab Soames himself had nothing to say, at least not to Matthews.

Hal Chrichton leaned in the front door of the office and said, "He got a lawyer yet?"

"Not yet."

"You let me speak to him, Reed?"

"If you want to. He probably doesn't have any money."

Chrichton, a man scarred by childhood chicken pox, smiled with piss-yellow teeth. "Yep, but think of all the publicity I'll get when I prove he's innocent."

"How do you know he's innocent? You haven't even talked to him yet."

"I've got a feeling about this one."

"'A feeling.' I hate to tell you, Hal, but I don't think that's admissible in court."

"It will be when I get through with old Judge Hoover." He was a tall, dapper man and he moved smoothly, a talent he'd picked up losing several dozen cases over the years. He was the worst lawyer in the county but he worked for free. "You going to unlock his cell and let me in?"

"I figured I'd just let you gnaw through the bars."

"Sarcastic devil this morning, aren't you, Sheriff?"

"Just where lawyers are concerned."

There was a tiny room about twice the size of a small closet where prisoners were questioned and where lawyers met prisoners. Matthews led Chrichton there. A window high in the ceiling lent the place a dusty luminescence.

"I could sure go for a cup of coffee, Sheriff."

"I could sure go for some gold bullion, myself."

Chrichton smiled. "All right if I get my own?"

"Bring a cup for Soames. With his hangover, he'll need it for sure." He went to get the prisoner.

Matthews was finishing up his coffee in Wymer's Café. He usually took a break mid-morning. He liked the coffee and the relaxation. And it gave folks a chance to come over and talk to him in an informal way. His position here was an elective one. He'd resented that fact at first, but now that he'd been in the job for a few years, he saw that elective office was the best way to serve. If people kept electing you, it generally meant that they liked you more than not. They at least liked you more than any of the people running against you, anyway. And you couldn't get much done if people didn't support you.

The one thing he was trying to do was stay neutral in the upcoming mayoral election. Mayor Ken Thomas had been hinting that he wanted a formal endorsement from Matthews. But the lawman found the mayor cynical, manipulative, and selfish. If something happened to be good for both him and the town, the mayor would do it. But if it was only good for the town and not the mayor, there was a good chance it would never get done.

"Morning, Sheriff."

Matthews looked up to see Roy Fuller, the accountant and business adviser to Vernon Davies—who just happened to be the father of Karen Davies, the woman Matthews was uselessly in love with—stop by the table. Fuller apparently couldn't wait to get outside to put his obviously new bowler on. He slipped it on right here and right now.

"Morning, Roy."

"Terrible thing." He didn't need to say what terrible thing he was referring to. This morning, there was only one terrible thing.

"It sure is." Matthews had never especially liked Fuller. He had the sense that Fuller lived in a world of numbers and abstractions. Human experience didn't seem to be quite as real to him as his accounting books. Even the way he'd said, "Terrible thing." A rote, blood-less comment.

Fuller nodded and walked to the front door of the café.

Frank Giff was a desk clerk from one of the hotels. He was one of those men whose features suggested that he might have some colored blood in him. Matthews had been in towns where this would have kept a man from getting any "white" jobs. But Giff didn't seem to have any problems. He was smart, hardworking, and a good family man. As far as Matthews knew, nobody in town had ever given him grief with the exception of two drifters. Matthews had knocked their heads together and run them out of town.

"Morning, Sheriff."

"Morning, Frank."

"You asked me once to tell you if we got any Pinkertons in town."

"Why don't you sit down, Frank?"

"I guess I could, I've got a couple minutes left on my break, anyway."

Frank Giff was a thin man in a Sears-catalog brown suit with white shirt, celluloid collar, and a tie three shades darker brown than his suit. He wore wire-rim glasses behind which rested two large, dark, intelligent eyes.

Giff took out his pipe. He didn't light it, just drew on it to absorb the sweet damp taste that resided in the bowl and stem.

"He arrived last night," Giff said. "Name's Carney. Dwight Carney. He goes maybe six foot. Tall fella. And stout. Nose looks like he might've done some boxing in his life."

"He tell you he was with the Pinkertons?"

"Left his business card. Asked me if I knew Vernon Davies. I told him, sure, Davies was an important man, everybody knew him. He said that if I saw Vernon Davies to give him this card. He put a little X up in the corner."

"An X?"

"Figured it was some kind of signal. A special card. I give this to Davies and Davies gives it to him when they meet. This way Carney knows that it's really Davies."

"I guess that makes sense. But it seems like an awful lot of trouble. Why not just go to Davies's house?"

Giff smiled. "Now there I can't help you."

"So have you seen Davies?"

"About twenty minutes ago. Came up to the desk and

asked if anybody'd left anything for him. I gave him the card."

"He say anything about it?"

"He looked nervous."

"Before or after he got the card?"

"Both. He usually swaggers a little. You know how Davies is. He wants you to know he's important. But not this morning. He just hurried in, looking around like somebody might be watching him or something."

"So he just took the card and left?"

"Pretty much."

"Have you seen this Carney yet today?"

"No. Either he left the hotel before I got there or he's still up in his room."

"It's going on eleven. He must be a late sleeper if he's still up there."

"Could be he had a long trip here and he's sleeping in."

"Could be."

"But I'd be careful around him. He doesn't look real friendly." Giff pulled his watch out of his vest pocket. "Well, there I go. Got to get back to it. Good luck with the Pinkerton."

Matthews didn't like Pinkertons operating in his town. He could give you a half dozen logical-sounding reasons for this, but what it came down to was Matthews's vanity. The strongest reason was that private operatives often proved violent or corrupt. But what he didn't like was the idea that one of his own townspeople would have to go around him to get something done. Weren't his sheriffing skills good enough? He liked to think he could deal competently with just about any problem.

Vanity. He didn't have much of it and was ashamed of the little he had. But where private operatives were concerned, he couldn't seem to admit that sometimes there were good reasons for private citizens to hire private operatives—and to admit that they had every right to do so.

Maybe it's time I deal with this, he thought. *Maybe I should find this Carney and tell him that I'm willing to help him any way I can.*

He realized that in a perverse way, his new attitude was just another form of vanity. He liked to think of himself as a fair and open-minded man. He disliked those lawmen who ran their towns like little kings. So what he was doing was weighing which form of vanity was more important to him. If he welcomed the man, he'd prove to himself that he was fair-minded. Was being fair-minded more fulfilling than the secret pleasure of running private ops out just about as soon as they got here?

He liked the sound of being fair-minded.

There goes Reed Matthews, a fair-minded man. Yeah, that had a nice sound to it, didn't it? In fact, that might be a line—that fair-minded thing—for the posters come election next time.

He wouldn't enjoy meeting this Carney and pretending that he was willing to help him in any way he could . . . but what the hell. He had to now that he'd been running that "fair-minded" thing around in his brain.

A few minutes later, he made his way to the hotel where Frank Giff worked.

SIX

"YOU ALL RIGHT, Dad?"

"I'm fine," Vernon Davies said.

But both of them knew it was a lie.

Davies was sitting on the front veranda of his Spanish-style home, one of the most envied places in town due to the careful magnificence of its making. The stucco walls cast off pure white light and the rich red of the roof tiles took in the radiance of the sun's rays, seeming all the richer for the absorption. The grounds were immaculate on this heady fall day.

Karen Davies was a slender young woman with a ridiculously beautiful face. A face without a bad angle, a face that required no fussing or tricks with makeup, a face that was as angelic frowning as it was smiling. The townsfolk always said the same thing, though: If only she didn't have that long scar down her left cheek, she'd be perfect. She sat down next to her father and said, "I heard you all night. Up and down."

"That's nothing new."

He spoke in the same dismissive tone he used whenever his employees on the short-line railroad wanted his time. Her father hated explaining himself to anybody. Under any circumstances. Ever. He and Mom had had many, many fights about this.

Then he softened his tone: "I'm fine, Sheriff."

"Sheriff?"

"That's what you sound like. All these questions."

"I simply asked," she said, holding her temper back, "how you were doing. I'm sorry to intrude on your valuable time. I'm worried about you, Dad—please forgive me."

He laughed. "Every time you get sarcastic, I hear your mom in your voice."

"Dad, all I'm trying to do—"

He reached across to her chair and patted her hand. "I know, honey. And I appreciate your concern."

"Ever since you got that letter—"

His smile vanished, as did his momentary gentle mood. "What the hell do you know about a letter?"

"I brought it to you, remember?"

Her father put in only three days a week. He'd left the daily workings of his rail line to the man he continually and contemptuously called "the college boy," Roy Fuller. But Fuller was hardly a boy. He was in his early forties and had a wife and two children.

Davies had made most of his fortune in the fur trade. He had always been a virile and perceptive businessman, but the fur trade shifted its preferences so often, no one man could work the market as he once had. In less than thirty years the trade had shifted through beaver, buffalo, raccoon, and now, just lately, from seal fur.

"I bring you the mail every morning you're home, Dad. Remember? I handed you several envelopes. You spotted something amiss with one of them right away. You went in the den and locked the door. About five minutes later—just about the time it would take you to read the letter—you exploded. You started ranting. And you spent practically the whole day locked in there getting drunk on brandy. You may not remember, but I do. And you haven't had a good night's sleep ever since. And you've been a bear to be around."

He stood up. He always wore dark suits to hide his heft. Hiding behind a barn, he could hide his heft. He'd bloomed that big in the past five years. "Forget about that letter, honey. I don't want you involved in this in any way."

At the time of Mom's death, she'd seen tears standing in her father's eyes. They glistened in them now.

He reached down and took her hand with a tenderness that moved her even more than his tears. She'd never seen him look so old or vulnerable. He wouldn't look much different from this lying in his coffin.

"You've got a curiosity that scares me sometimes, honey. And this is one time I don't want you to do anything about it. You can't help me with this. This is something I have to handle by myself. I'm pretty sure I can take care of it, but I've got to figure a few things out first. I was supposed to meet somebody an hour ago and he didn't show up. I don't know what that means. But I need to find out."

"Dad, please let me help you."

"You can't help me," he said. "You can only get yourself tangled up in something that you don't want to know about—believe me." He slipped his hand from hers and stood up straight. He looked drained, exhausted, gray. "I want your word on this."

"If it means that much to you, all right, Dad. You have my word. But I'm scared."

The gentleness was gone from his eyes and voice. He was as hard and angry now as he was when he was forced to go after a business competitor. "I said I'll take care of it and I will. You probably don't think I can defend myself anymore. But I'm not as old and feeble as I might have seemed since that letter came. I'm going to handle this the same way I would've when I was thirty years old. And that you can count on."

She smiled at her father with great fondness, forgetting the letter and the meeting he'd just mentioned. She reached up and took his hand and said, "Of course you'll handle it, Dad. You always do and it won't be any different now."

"That's all you need to remember, honey. 'It won't be any different now.' The exact words you said." He bussed her on the cheek. "And now I've got some advice for you. Forget how that bastard Marcus Evans treated you and get yourself married to Reed Matthews as soon as possible. I'm almost embarrassed for him, the way he looks at you sometimes. All cow-eyed. Just because your first marriage turned out bad doesn't mean this one will."

She'd married a dashing Army captain when she was nineteen. She was vain enough to think that he'd been all caught up in her looks and the fact that so many young men found her not only pretty but a good companion— fun and smart and loyal.

"Is that an order?" She smiled. "About marrying Reed?"

"I just wish you were young enough to still *take* orders. I'd give a couple of other ones, too, while I was at it."

He nodded and walked slowly into the cool house of shadows. She sat in the chair watching birds and butterflies frolic.

She had only one thought. She doubted that her father had destroyed the mysterious letter. As soon as she was sure that he was napping, she was going to get into his den and find it.

After he'd knocked twice, Matthews put his ear to the door of Room 207 and listened. And heard nothing. If the Pinkerton man was inside, he was sleeping. But Matthews didn't hear any snoring, either, or the sound a bed makes when a sleeper moves around on it.

There was a little matter of illegally entering somebody's room. A person could protest if he wanted to and put the lawman in some legal jeopardy.

Matthews turned the doorknob. He wouldn't be in any legal jeopardy this time. The door wasn't locked.

He eased the door open with his left hand. His right rode the handle of his holstered Colt. You never knew what you were going to find behind a closed door.

A cardinal sat on the windowsill. It made merry noises. Seemed the birds were just about as happy with this fine fall day as the humans.

The room was neat and orderly and empty.

He started searching the room. Carefully, so the Pinkerton man wouldn't know right away that anybody had been in here.

Familiar stuff. Extra clothes. A couple of books. Tobacco pouch. A brochure about the Pinkertons with boasts and promises no organization could ever live up to.

He found three photographs. The same heavy, nose-broken, balding man with the full beard appeared in two of them. This was the Pinkerton Dwight Carney, no doubt. In each of the photographs — stiffly posed — a pretty girl of five or six sat on one knee while the Pinkerton's bowler sat on the other. The only difference in the photographs was that in the second one the Pinkerton's cravat had been straightened up. The third photograph was of the little girl alone. Looking at these, he imagined that the Pinkerton probably got pretty lonely for his little girl, traipsing all over the countryside the way private ops usually do.

He spent another ten minutes in the room but found nothing else of interest.

In the lobby, he spotted Giff at the front desk and walked over. "You hear anything more on Carney?"

"I guess he asked Clarence — you know, the colored janitor — I guess he asked Clarence if he knew where the old riverboat dock was. The deserted one, I suppose he meant."

"When was this?"

"Clarence said it was this morning. When Carney was leaving the hotel."

"Thanks, Giff."

"My pleasure, Sheriff."

The original dock for steamboats had been vacated because there wasn't enough room for expansion. Warehouses took up most of the space an expanded dock would need. So the steamboat company that controlled the dock built new facilities upriver.

Just before noon, Matthews stood on the original dock, looking out at the raw, powerful span of river. The Colorado was a pisser, no doubt about it. It gave captains and crews every kind of menace and thrill they could possibly want—the kinds of menaces and thrills dime novelists thrived on. You wanted Indian attacks, you got 'em; you wanted water so turbulent it had sunk even the proudest of steamboats, no problem; you wanted winters so bitter and violent that a few passengers actually froze to death in their shabby little cabins—the Colorado gave you all of this on a regular basis.

And yet it was still as thrilling to Matthews as railroads were to most people. The huge boats, the colorful crews and passengers, the festive air that accompanied many of the landings—he always felt like a boy when he was around steamboats. He'd never gotten over his childhood thrill of them.

The dock was empty. Muddy river water washed up against it. River birds soared and dove after food. A stray dog took a leak against a post. When school let out, this entire area would be flooded not with water but with kids. The deserted buildings were a great playground, even though they were boarded up and locked. But kids being kids, they had no trouble figuring out a way in. A couple times a day, one of Matthews's deputies would come down here and run the kids off. But in fifteen minutes, they'd be back, much against the will of both the parents and the law.

He wondered if Carney's meeting with Vernon Davies had taken place. Then he wondered what it had been about.

He spent a few minutes letting his senses satisfy themselves with the scents of river and sunlight and the particular smell, not at all unpleasant, of wood that had been washed by river water for many years. He watched the stray dog. Now there was a life. Trotting around all day, looking for some kind of adventure. Every once in a while, Matthews found himself wishing he was ten years old again. Ten had been just about the best year of his life.

He walked back to the center of town.

SHERIFF was four small offices up front and four jail cells in back. The only times all the cells got used up was on weekends, and then the prisoners ran to drunk-and-disorderlies and vandals who'd smashed store windows while in the noisy throes of whiskey exuberance. Anybody more dangerous than that, the occasional bank robber or the occasional killer, meant that a crowd of young boys would gather outside the jail along the west wall and look at the bars high up near the roof. They read about killers and they of course talked about killers, but how often did you actually get to be right outside the jail from one? The trouble was, these weren't the killers of dime novels, those fancy highwaymen who held romantic fascination for people of all kinds. These were usually men who'd stove in their wives' heads with cast-iron frying pans; or drunkenly stomped to death the man they'd lost a few drunken dollars to in a card game; or the predator who raped just before he killed. You saw them in the sunlight and all the legends and myths about criminals came crashing down—they were everyday, common men who looked variously defiant and angry, or ashamed or forlorn. A few of them would hang themselves in jail before the time came for their trials. They almost weren't worth waiting around to see.

It was a morning of small surprises. A lawyer showing up for Ab Soames; and now a familiar-looking business card on his desk.

DWIGHT CARNEY
Pinkerton Investigative Agency
Denver, Colorado

The card also carried the business address plus the symbol of the eye that peered out at you, the symbol that got Pinkertons called "private eyes" by some newspapermen.

He picked up the card and went up to where Butch Long was sitting at the front desk writing out his time sheet. Butch was a good deputy when he was awake. People liked him. He was a quiet, mild man who was good at the small things—there was, for instance, no man so skilled at getting a kitten down from a tree. He was also accomplished at carrying groceries for old women, fixing wheels for the wagons of little girls and boys, and calming tempers of hotheads. He was so good at this that if there'd been a national temper-cooling award, Butch would win flat out. Butch's problem was that he could and did sleep whenever he got the opportunity—and if an opportunity didn't present itself, ole Butch was willing to create one. He slept in closets, under desks, in sheds, barns, buggies, and—if absolutely necessary—right at his desk. Matthews should have fired him, of course, long ago, but Butch had two tiny daughters with a congenital disease that would kill them before they reached ten. How do you fire a man like that? Especially when he was such a decent fella?

Butch, happily, was awake.

"This Carney drop his card off personally?"

Butch was a round, heavily bearded man who usually won any contest involving strength. His biceps were half as thick as most men's thighs. "Yep. Nice fella, too."

"He tell you he was a Pinkerton?"

"Uh-huh. He said he couldn't tell me any more. Said he was here working on a confidential matter but wanted to stop in and introduce himself to the local law. He said a lot of Pinkertons are doin' that today, stoppin' in and introducin' themselves that way."

"I wonder what Alan Pinkerton thinks of that," Matthews said. "He thinks most of us are rubes." He smiled. "And maybe he's got somethin' there."

"Speak for yourself." Butch laughed. "Myself personally, I'm a sophisticated gent."

"Yeah, just like me." Matthews tapped the card

against his thumbnail. "He say if he'd stop back or anything?"

"Nope. Just left his card. Said he'd probably run into you sometime in town here. Said if you had any questions for him he was over at the hotel."

"Guess I'll go back and see the prisoner."

Butch made a sympathetic face. "Funny to say it, but I sort of like the fella. I brought him his breakfast and we got to talkin'. I mean, I ain't sayin' he didn't kill the old man. But he's still sort of nice to talk to. Quiet and all. I told him I'd send a priest or a parson over but he said no, that he had his own way of dealin' with things like that. Seems like a lonely sort of fella."

"That's the hell of it sometimes," Matthews said. "You get decent people who do the wrong thing and then you wonder sometimes what happened to them. Their whole lifetime and for just a minute or two they do something terrible. And it changes them forever. They spend the rest of their lives regretting it."

"Brought you some tobacco."

Ab Soames was the only prisoner in the jail. He sat on the cot and watched as Matthews opened the cell door, came in, locked it behind him. Then he tossed Soames the fixings.

"Thanks," Soames said. "That's sure a nice deputy you got."

"Butch?"

"Yeah, guess that was his name. He was tellin' me about his little girls. How they'll be dead pretty soon and all. Don't know how a man could live knowin' something like that."

"You getting food and everything all right?"

"Yeah, everything's fine."

"How's your memory coming along?"

Soames shrugged. "I still don't remember killing him. Which means I don't think I did. I mean, you kill a man, no matter how drunk you are, you'd think you'd remember."

"You'd think. But there're some men who can't remember two, three days at a time."

Soames watched him with frightened blue eyes. "You keep talking like that, you just might convince me that I actually killed him."

"How'd it go with your lawyer?"

"He any good?"

"He's all right. He's not the best. But since you don't have any money, he's the best we can get you."

"He keeps saying that I could probably get out of hanging if I plead guilty and just hold to that I was drunk and didn't know what I was doing."

"That's called diminished capacity."

"Yeah," Soames said, "that's what he said. Diminished capacity. You think I should do that? I don't want to hang. My stomach—" He touched his belly. "It just starts to burn when I think of hanging."

"I can't advise you on that. It's up to you."

"I just keep thinking that I didn't kill my uncle. That's the only thing that keeps me from pleading guilty and just getting everything over with and going right to prison."

"That's what he wants you to do?"

"He says he doesn't want to see me hang and that we haven't got much of a defense."

"But you think there's a chance you didn't kill him."

"There's more than a chance, Sheriff. I'm almost positive I didn't kill him. If I killed him, I'd remember it. Maybe not the whole thing. But I'd remember a little something of it. A little something, at least. So if I plead guilty—what if I serve twenty, thirty years and then they find out I really didn't kill him at all?"

"Or what if they hang you and then find out you really didn't kill him at all?"

"Yeah," Soames said quietly. "That's what I keep thinking. That's why I'm inclined to plead guilty. At least, part of the time I'm inclined that way. He says he'll talk to the county attorney and try to work something out as soon as I give him the word." He laughed sourly. "It's funny. Every time I start to think about this, I get a real bad headache. A real bad headache. Because I don't like either choice."

"I wish I could help you, but you've got to make that decision alone."

Soames looked up to him with his liquor-ravaged face. He was an old man and not yet thirty. Only the eyes, the yearning, scared eyes, were young. He said, "Just tell me what you'd do in my place, Sheriff. I won't tell anybody what you say. Please? I'd really appreciate it."

Matthews sighed. "Well, to me, it's real simple. To be on the safe side, I'd plead guilty and go to prison. There's always the chance that we'll find out something later on, just like you say. But if you hang, no matter what we find out later on sure isn't going to do you any good."

"I guess that's your answer, huh?"

"Yeah, I guess it is."

SEVEN

HE SAT IN on the inquest. The small courtroom was crowded so he didn't feel conspicuous. He knew there was some risk in this, the same as there had been some risk in being in the tree after the murder at Soames's mansion last night, but he wanted to keep apprised of everything. He needed to make some plans.

The judge was an irritable man. Displeased, he sounded more like a scold than an impartial jurist. Several of the onlookers smirked when the judge got angry.

A true cross section of the town seemed to be here, from the cold-eyed businessmen to the somewhat intimidated gaggle of laborers and farmers. You could tell the sheep men. Nobody wanted to sit anywhere near them because of the stench.

He watched the sheriff with particular interest. Reed Matthews sat in the witness box relating what he'd seen last night. He followed the county coroner and Martha Soames, who broke into tears; Tyrell the butler, who seemed disdainful of the whole process; and the maid, Ernestine Prowell, who, like Martha Soames, cried a good deal.

"I understand you have a prisoner in the jail," the county attorney said. He was an efficient-looking man, Donald Tavesty, and a man curiously ashamed of his thumbs. For most of the hour-long inquest, he kept them tucked away in the pockets of his vest. This was his third two-year term as county attorney. It was said that Tavesty kept getting reelected because he was able as a Methodist to put together the Methodist vote with the Presbyterian vote, the two largest blocs of votes in town. The newspaper had run an editorial condemning such "jealous speculation." Tavesty was their man, the newspaper staff being mostly Methodist, and they editorialized, "This isn't Chicago. Men here are elected purely on ability." They did not point out that Tavesty had lost better than fifty percent of his cases.

"Yessir."

"His name, please."

"Ab Soames."

"Ab?"

"Abner."

"I see. And you have evidence against this man?"

"Yes." Matthews's lips formed an almost invisible expression of displeasure. Efficient as Tavesty was, he occasionally went theatrical on you and played to the crowd. His thespian inclinations—inclinations he shared with his equally thespian wife—could be seen full-bore at the annual Methodist Spring Community Fest where Tavesty frequently took the role of a town pioneer. He would have probably kept his thumbs tucked away then, too, but the buckskins he always wore lacked those little pockets.

"Would you share that evidence with us?" Tavesty said dramatically, addressing the crowd.

Matthews went through everything he'd collected. He also went through a review of Ab Soames's drinking history and his relationship with his uncle.

The efficient county attorney looked exceptionally pleased. This kind of self-indulgent behavior had nothing to do with a real inquest. A real inquest dealt simply with cause of death. If homicide, then a grand jury was impaneled. But the efficient Mr. Tavesty found such proceedings dull—he wanted to keep his thespian talents sharp for the spring festival—and so he frequently informed the court whom he considered guilty and started then and there building his case against the man. The judge didn't mind a little drama, either. Kept him awake, anyway, him given to the heavy lunches of his German wife, which left him logy in the afternoon sessions.

"I think it's pretty clear what we're dealing with here, Your Honor," Tavesty said to the bench.

The judge nodded.

"We have premeditated murder and we have a very likely suspect," Tavesty went on.

The judge nodded again. Dumplings for lunch were not a good idea. Especially when they were a-swim in heavy gravy. He tapped his sternum. The older he got, the more unstable his digestive system became. He felt as if he had a baseball stuck in his esophagus.

"Very good, Mr. Tavesty," the judge said, suppressing a belch. "Do you have anything further to add, Sheriff?"

Matthews said, "No, sir," in a distracted way that made the judge even more dyspeptic. He expected the full attention of those in the witness box.

But Matthews was watching the three men in the front row of the courtroom.

Vernon Davies, Hector Nolan, Bryce Harlow. Three of Gerald Soames's best friends, three of the most successful men in this part of the state, and three men he could never recall seeing at an inquest before. Certainly, they would be interested in what had happened to their friend. They'd want justice, quick justice, and a return to civic normalcy. In addition to missing their friend, they'd also be well aware that a murder never did a town any good. It left a faint taint on the town that took a long time to fade.

Their demeanor only reenforced Matthews's curiosity. They kept shifting in their seats; two of them were sweating unduly in the cool courtroom, which was sixty degrees at most; and Hector Nolan was attacking his fingernails the way he attacked corn on the cob at autumn festivals.

Matthews forced his attention back to the judge. "No, sir, I don't have anything to add."

"You already said that, Sheriff."

"Oh." Matthews felt his cheeks flush. Some of the people in the courtroom snickered.

"Thank you, Sheriff," Tavesty said.

As he was standing up in the box, ready to take his seat again, Matthews noticed the man in the back. Short, slight, and somehow familiar. Dark inexpensive suit. There was an air of isolation about the man and not just because he sat alone in the back. There are some people who give off a loneliness that threatens other people, who instinctively understand that isolated people are sometimes dangerous, that the reason for their isolation can be sinister. Hoboes, gunfighters, and insane people were three categories of such people. This young man didn't seem to be any of the three, but he definitely gave off a sense of alienation and mystery. Matthews, being a good lawman, wondered who he was and why he was at the inquest.

Matthews walked from the witness stand to the front of the courtroom. He sat near the three businessmen he'd been watching. Up this close, they looked even more agitated. They gaped at him from time to time, looking as if they wanted to ask him something.

At the end of the inquest, Matthews made for the back of the courtroom. He was still curious about the young man who'd sat in the back. But by the time he made his way through the clusters of people talking and blocking the aisle, he didn't see the young man anywhere.

He stood in the sunlight at the foot of the courthouse steps, watching Davies, Nolan, and Harlow exit the building. They'd usually be talking with great enthusiasm and animation. They did a lot of land speculation — this was the time to buy with recession rolling across the land — and could be seen exploding two or three times a day with enormous enthusiasm for a certain stretch of land that they could get for a very good price.

They were silent, somber, as they descended the steps. They didn't look around, they didn't even acknowledge him, though they passed within a few feet of him.

Matthews wondered what the hell was going on with them. He seemed to be missing some vital fact about the murder of their friend Gerald Soames. Their appearance at the inquest was odd enough, their behavior even odder.

He was tempted to confront them, but then remembered he was going to find Dwight Carney.

EIGHT

THERE WERE SOME logical places to look for Carney. His hotel, the café, the telegraph office to see if he'd received or sent anything, the two most respectable saloons. Matthews didn't find him in any of these places.

What he did find was a perfectly good excuse to talk to one of the three men who'd sat so dourly at the inquest this morning.

Vernon Davies had made his fortune early on. He'd had his ostentatious years — had even talked of political office for a time — but then he'd become invisible to the town. No more public walks with his fancy cane; no more baritone solos at the church; no more stem-winding talks to his lessers at the Odd Fellows. This had all happened within the last decade or so. At first the speculation had been that he might be sick. A lot of people who'd been pronounced seriously ill drew into themselves. But if he was dying, he was a long time leaving. And when you looked at him on one of his rare strolls through town, he looked just fine for a man of his age and build.

Then there was his daughter. . . .

That spring, Karen Davies took strolls along the river at night. She helped out with the nurse shortage at the hospital. Her strolls were part of her break. He'd gotten to know her when she sat down with him on a bench overlooking the moon-spangled river. And then he fell in love with her. It was strange. One day she was just a pretty girl, and the next day—or night along the river to be exact—he found himself exuberant, sick, and scared all at the same time—a sure sign he'd fallen in love. . . .

He knocked.

She came to the door a few moments later. "Well, talk about surprises."

"Hi, Karen. Good to see you."

She smiled. "But I'll bet it's not me you're here to see."

"Not entirely."

"Not at all, you mean. But I can take it. I'm a big girl."

In the light of late day, her gentle beauty had the effect of a sentimental painting on him. Even the slash of scarring seemed a natural part of her. "You look great."

"Thanks," she said. "And so do you actually."

He hadn't talked to her for a few days. He'd started asking her to marry him again, and she always pulled back when he did that. Her first marriage had destroyed her faith in relationships and there wasn't anything he could do about it.

She stepped out of the way and invited him in. "All right if I put you in the den? Carmella's cleaning the house today. She works very fast and resents anybody who gets in her way."

"She sounds dangerous."

"That's no joke. Make her mad sometime and see what happens. I've always felt bad about having servants. It just seems so demeaning to them. We didn't always have them. I can actually remember when my parents were poor. But Carmella got me over worrying about servants."

"Oh? How'd she do that?"

Karen laughed. It was a light, perfect, female laugh. "Easy. I take orders from her."

The den smelled of pipe smoke. Vernon Davies sat at his desk. He didn't look happy, didn't look well. He'd acted agitated in the courtroom. Now he looked too drained and exhausted to summon up agitation. Bloated, pale, even forlorn.

Karen registered the same reaction to her father that Matthews did. She glanced at Reed and shook her head.

"I'll go out and ask Carmella what she wants me to do," she said, hoping for a moment of humor. Her father didn't seem to hear her at all.

She shut the door quietly behind her.

"I'm afraid I can only give you a few minutes," Davies said, glancing at Matthews with watery eyes. He nodded to a leather chair. Matthews sat down. "I'm tired. Maybe I'm coming down with something."

Matthews had learned long ago that the best way to handle delicate matters was to approach them directly. No amenities. No stalling. No hedging. He said, "There's a Pinkerton man in town name of Dwight Carney. I'm looking for him. Thought maybe you could help me, Vernon."

Davies found an unexpected load of anger. He sat up straighter; his watery eyes flashed with hard anger. He said, "What the hell's that supposed to mean?"

"Means just what it seems, Vernon. I'm trying to find him and I know you know something about him."

"Now how would you know that?"

"You don't really expect me to tell you. Do you?"

Davies's temper diminished a bit. "Aren't I entitled to my privacy?"

"Of course."

"Then by what right are you in my house asking me a question like that?" His pipe had gone out. He struck a match against a strip of flint and then brushed tobacco flecks from the same clothes he'd worn to the inquest.

"I'm just wondering why a Pinkerton man comes to town at the same time Gerald Soames gets murdered," Matthews said.

"You've already arrested somebody."

"That doesn't mean he's guilty."

"You're in the habit of arresting people you don't think are guilty?"

"Look," Matthews said. "There may be no connection between your Pinkerton man and the murder at all.

There probably isn't. But would you do me the favor of telling me where I can find him?"

"No, I won't tell you because it's none of your damned business. You can't burst into somebody's house and make demands like this."

"I'm not making demands, Vernon. I'm asking you to do me a favor. All I need you to do is tell me that you invited him here for your own reasons and that those reasons had nothing to do with Soames."

Davies's pipe went out again. He made an intricate and extremely slow production of lighting it. He'd decided to start irritating Matthews the way Matthews was irritating him. "Do you know anything about how Pinkertons work, Matthews?"

"Pretty much."

"They don't hold much truck with regular lawmen and they prefer not to work with them if possible."

"Not so much anymore, Vernon. In fact, your Pinkerton man made a point of stopping by my office while I was out. Said he wanted to introduce himself."

"Now that's a load of shit and you know it."

"Afraid not, Vernon. He even left his business card."

The big man sighed. The anger that had animated him for a few minutes had drained from him. He looked old and tired and irritated and vaguely frightened. "I need to think about some things, Matthews."

"Believe it or not, Vernon, I didn't come here to upset you. I came here to help you."

The anger returned for a brief moment. "That may not have been your intention, Matthews. But that's the result you got. I'm not at my best or I'd physically throw you out."

Matthews stood up. "C'mon, Vernon. Let's keep this civil."

Now Davies stood up, imposing even with diminished strength. He shocked Matthews with his smile. "Now that that's behind us, when're you going to marry my daughter?"

"You changed subjects pretty fast. And why would you want her to marry somebody you want to throw off your property?"

"Hell, I was just mad. I don't like you poking around in my business. But that doesn't mean you wouldn't make her a good husband."

Matthews laughed. "You're a hard man to keep up with sometimes."

"That's why I'm rich. Be sure and spend a little time with Karen while you're here."

This was the only time Matthews didn't take the time to look over all the refinements Karen had made to the house. The old man's taste ran to the garish, Karen's to more subdued Eastern styles. The Persian rugs, the grand piano, the window seats, the ferns and flowers, even the formidable tomcat known as Lazy had changed the place completely over the past two years. Karen always laughed about how her father grumbled over every change. Left up to him, the walls would have been covered with moose heads, the magazine racks stuffed with copies of the *Police Gazette.*

She waited for him on the front porch, sitting on the porch railing. "I don't know which is worse—him trying to throw you out. Or him playing matchmaker."

"You heard, huh?"

"Heard? You could hear my father three houses away. Especially when he's mad."

"He's not helping me, Karen, and I need help."

"You asked him about the Pinkerton man. That much I heard. I was snooping."

He watched her for a reaction to what he said next. "I don't suppose you know anything about this Pinkerton?"

"Not really. Dad's been very secretive lately."

"I may have an innocent man in jail."

"I'd help if I could."

"I know." He walked over to a chair and picked up his Stetson. "I need to get going."

"I thought Dad told you to spend a little time with me."

He hesitated, thinking over how to express what he felt. "We're a long ways down the road, Karen. You know I want to marry you. I can't turn back to just being friends."

She touched his arm, kissed him tenderly on the cheek. "I'm trying to think it through, Reed. I'm scared is all."

There wasn't much to say to that. He cinched on his hat and left.

NINE

WHEN HE GOT back to his office, the first thing Matthews asked about was the Pinkerton man. Still no sign of him.

Matthews spent an hour looking over and signing documents of all kinds that pertained to town business. None of it bothered him except the foreclosure sales one of his men would have to oversee. Between recessions, not enough rain, too much rain, too early a spring, too late a spring, and so on, farmers had a difficult time making any kind of living. And when banks were hard-pressed as they were now—as always, there was talk in Washington about regulating some of the more excessive of bank practices and thereby helping to stabilize the economy—the banks always got downright mercenary with their smallest customers. Funny how they'd let rich men twist the laws so that they came out all right no matter what their paper losses might total — but a family of four that worked a farm twelve, fourteen hours a day . . . they'd get kicked out of their home, driven to town to find jobs that would keep them unhappy the rest of their lives.

He was always in a sour mood when he dealt with foreclosure sales, and today was no different.

He was in no mood for Reverend Hovey.

The stiff, unpleasant man always irritated him by coming in the back door. He knew that if he came in the front door, whoever was on the front desk would lie and say that Sheriff Matthews wasn't in. So he'd taken to lurking in the barn in back and then scooting inside when he saw one of the deputies let himself in with a key.

He knocked sharply and said, "I'm afraid I don't have very good news for you, Sheriff."

"Gosh, now there's a surprise. You never seem to have good news for me, Reverend Hovey."

"I think there's a woman in this very town who has become a prostitute and is operating out of her tiny little flat."

The small, thin man in the clerical collar and black suit came into Matthews's office and sat down, unasked, across from the sheriff's desk.

"And who might that be, Reverend?"

"Helen Acry."

"Oh, for shit's sake, Reverend. And pardon my French. But Helen Acry is one of the most decent people in this town. She lives in her 'tiny little flat' as you call it because that's all she can afford since her husband got killed on the railroad. She's got two little ones to support and she works fifteen hours a day to keep them fed and clothed. You've told me some howlers before, Reverend. But this is too much."

"She lives right across the alley from the church. We see what goes on there."

"Well, I'm sure as hell not going to go over there and tell her I have a complaint that she's practicing prostitution."

"A man came to her place after midnight last night."

"That's not against the law."

"It *should* be against the law," the good reverend said. He was a champion of every so-called "conservative" cause that came up. He was against government on just about every level. The only thing he thought government should do was legislate morality—his kind of morality, of course. He didn't see any irony, let alone hypocrisy, in this—you stay out of my business, my government man, but go right ahead and poke your nose into everybody else's. He was the worst kind of citizen, the sort who stopped by the office once or twice a week to demand action for some boneheaded reason that was usually laughable.

"Well, maybe it *should* be against the law, Reverend, but right now it isn't and so there isn't anything I can do to help you."

"Not even if drunkards sleep off their good times right in the alley?"

"There's a drunkard in her alley?"

"There certainly is. He's the same man who came there so late last night. And he's still there in the alley."

"You checked him over?"

"Checked him over?"

"See that he's alive."

"Of course he's alive. He's just sated on whiskey and sin. Satan robs us of our God-given strength when we indulge in sins of lust."

"So you didn't check him out?"

"That's not my place."

"I thought you were a man of God. Sounds like something Jesus would've done, Reverend, at least seen if the man was sick and needed help."

"He's sick, all right, Sheriff. Sick in his mind and sick in his soul. Cavorting with prostitutes and getting so drunk that he sleeps it off in an alley. And I don't need any instructions from you on what Jesus would do. If I spent my days helping out riffraff, I'd never get anything else done."

"I'll have one of my deputies swing by there and check him out." He tapped the eraser of his pencil against the papers on his desk. "Now I have to get back to work."

"Is it too much to hope for that you'll arrest Helen Acry for prostitution?"

"Yes, Reverend," Matthews said, smiling with great—and hopefully grating—amusement. "It's too much to hope for. I won't say anything except 'hello' to Helen the next time I see her. Now please let me get back to my work."

The good reverend never looked happy when he left Matthews's office.

Today was no exception.

• • •

Of course, as far as that went, Matthews didn't look all that happy, either. He had a lawman's instinct for bad news and fifteen minutes later, as he knelt down next to the corpse, that instinct was borne out.

The "drunkard" that the reverend had told him about wasn't drunk at all. He was dead.

Matthews had found his Pinkerton man sprawled right out there in the sunny alley with three wee ones looking on.

"He stinks pretty bad," said a little girl with pigtails.

"Yes," said Matthews, "he sure enough does."

PART TWO

PART TWO

ONE

"YOU'D NEVER SEEN him before?"

"Never, Sheriff. Honest to God."

"Helen, please. Quit shaking. I'm not accusing you of anything."

"Them kids of mine—if I ever got hauled off to jail—"

She was pure prairie woman, worn and wan by age thirty, knuckles torn from hard water and hard work, attractive in her blue-eyed defiance that said that no matter what sort of obstacle was put in front of her, she was going to master it for the sake of her children. She put in fifteen-hour days and never complained.

Matthews had never seen her rattled or scared before. He felt ashamed that his badge would intimidate her like this. She didn't have furniture; she had crates of various sizes, some used as chairs, some used as tables. She sat

all faded gingham and fierce-eyed terror on the edge of
one of the crates. A chicken from her backyard had gotten in and walked around the dirt floor of her apartment.
Neither of them paid it much attention.

"I just don't want no trouble, Sheriff."

Poor people learned early on to be afraid of the law.
Some of the sheriffs Matthews had worked for, he could
see why. One man he worked for had a setup where he'd
take a man's wife back to his office if she couldn't make
her husband's bail. Then he'd get her to do a "favor," as
he called it. One night a woman started sobbing and said
she couldn't do it. Matthews heard her and went back to
check it out. His hatred of the sheriff had been boiling up
ever since he'd found out how he forced the women to
make "bail" as he called it, though few of the women
seemed to understand that bail was set by judges, not
sheriffs. But they were so intimidated they just went
along, afraid to ask questions or say no. But this one
night—Matthews kicked the door in and broke his boss's
nose with a single roundhouse punch. He tossed the
woman the keys, told her to let her husband out of the cell
and advise him not to get drunk and disorderly again, and
then he took the sheriff at gunpoint up the hill to where a
wealthy judge lived. He made the lawman tell the judge
how he'd been using the wives of men he arrested. The
judge ran him out of town on the spot. The judge then
asked if Matthews wanted the top man's job. But
Matthews had had enough of the town already. He de-
clined. When dawn came, he saddled up and rode away.

He got down on his haunches in front of Helen. His
knees cracked as he did this. He took her hands in his

and kissed her tenderly on the cheek. He had great admiration and affection for women like Helen. And here he was scaring the hell out of her.

She sat beneath a cheaply printed magazine page that depicted the Virgin Mary. It had been nailed to the wall.

He said, "Helen, I want you to listen to me, all right?"

Her entire body trembled. "All right."

"There's nothing for you to be afraid of."

"That minister told you stories about me, didn't he? They're not true, Sheriff."

"I know they're not, Helen. Nobody in this town would believe that of you. He spreads gossip about everybody."

"Religious men ought not to do that."

"No, they shouldn't, Helen." He paused. "But I need to ask you a question, Helen. All I need is a simple answer. All I need to know is the truth and I'm sure everything will be fine. All right?"

"I appreciate you being so nice and all."

He smiled. She hadn't quite quit trembling, but she was trembling a whole lot less. "So you ready for my question?"

"I know what it's gonna be, Sheriff."

"All right. Then just tell me."

"I don't know why he came here."

"How did he happen to come inside?"

"He knocked. Real franticlike. You know how they do sometimes. Real frantic. He was out of breath. He scared me. Me'n the boys was asleep over there." She indicated a wide shabby bed over in the corner. "You get woken up like that, you get scared."

"You sure do."

"I always keep my husband's knife on the floor next to the bed on account of something bad happening. And anyway, I took it and got out of bed. What I was mainly worried about was him wakin' the kids up. So I opened the door—I didn't even have a lantern lit—and he just jumped inside and put some money in my hand."

"Money?"

"Uh-huh. He said that somebody was followin' him and he wanted to 'lose them.' That's how he put it. 'Lose them.' I never heard that expression before."

"Then what happened, Helen?"

"He told me to go back to bed. He said he'd only be here a few minutes. He just wanted to wait until this person who was followin' him passed by. I suppose he thought the fella would think he lost him."

"He say anything about this fella?"

"Nope. Nothing."

"How long was he here?"

"Not very long. A couple of minutes was all. Like he said."

"He say anything else before he left?"

"Nope. He stood by that door there and kept it open a crack and I guess just waited till this fella ran past. That was the last I saw of him."

"Somebody killed him not far from here."

"I know. In the alley."

"Did you see him?"

"Nope. I usually walk the boys to school in the morning. We always walk the street way, not the alley way. But when I got back from school little Ardele—she's got blond hair and pigtails—she come over and told me there was a drunk man in the alley. I honestly never thought it was him. I just took her word for it that he was drunk."

"So he didn't give you anything but the money?"

"No."

"How much?"

"He give me two one-dollar bank notes. National ones."

"Lucky he didn't give you any wildcat money." Wildcat banks had started issuing their own currency over the past three decades and had damned near destroyed the economy. Now there were national bank notes to replace the state ones.

"I'm gonna save 'em. We're always runnin' low when other people're runnin' low. They can't afford to get no laundry done, so I'm out in the cold till they get back on their feet again."

He stood up and walked around the room. He looked at the chicken and the chicken looked back at him. It was sort of a staring contest. The chicken won.

He said, "If you think of anything he might've said— anything at all, even if it didn't make any sense—would you stop by my office and tell me?"

"Sure I will." She stood up now, too. "I'll put him in my prayers. Bet he had a family and everything, poor fella. Die like that in an alley. Nobody to help him."

"He was a Pinkerton. That can get to be pretty rough work sometimes. That's why I need to figure out what he was doing in town here. Somebody wasn't happy to see him."

"The man who was chasing him."

"Yeah," Matthews said. "The man who was chasing him."

The rest of the afternoon ran predictably. First came the mayor, who warned that the town would soon get the kind of violent reputation it had back when it was a boomtown. Then came a group of church ladies who were worried about the town's children playing. Was it safe? What was Matthews going to do about the two killings? And finally the newspaper in the chubby form of the publisher's son arrived, ready for Matthews to make some kind of statement. He was disappointed with the only statement the lawman would give him. "This is still a safe town. And I don't know as yet if the murder of Gerald Soames had anything to do with the murder of this Dwight Carney, the Pinkerton man. And as for Ab Soames, he'll stay right where he's at for the time being until I can figure things out. And that's all I've got to say."

As soon as the publisher's son left, Matthews poured a couple cups of coffee and went back to the cells. Ab Soames was still the only prisoner. He was sleeping, snoring.

"Wake up, Ab."

The liquor was wearing off. Ab came up as if he'd been stabbed. You could see his momentary disorientation. Then his eyes settled on Matthews and the coffee.

"Take these damned things," Matthews said, pushing the coffee cups through the slot in the jail door. "Stuff's scalding my hands. I spilled it all over my hands."

A few minutes later, they faced each other in the cell, drinking their coffee.

"I don't think you killed him, but I think you know who did."

"Hell, Sheriff, if I knew that, I'd tell you."

"You were drunk. A lot of times when you're drunk like that, you lose memory for a couple of days but then it comes back. There's a good chance you knew who was in that room with your uncle."

"God, I wish I could remember."

"Maybe you will. Just spend a little time trying to put the whole day and night together. You may not remember everything, but maybe you'll remember enough that some pieces of memory'll come back here and there."

"You really don't think I did it?"

"No, I don't."

"I appreciate that."

"But that doesn't mean anything, Ab. Right now the county attorney could make a good case against you. All I could say on your side is that I don't think you did it. But that sure wouldn't hold up very well in court."

"No, I guess it wouldn't." Ab's expression alternated between hope and despair.

"You're the only one who can help figure this thing out. I'm thinking that whoever killed your uncle also killed the Pinkerton man."

"Yeah, I heard about that."

"They're connected."

"Well, if that's the case, are you going to let me go?"

"Can't, Ab. I'm sorry. The county attorney would be all over me. I live here; this is my home. I don't want to be accused of letting 'dangerous criminals' roam the streets."

"But I'm not a dangerous criminal."

"You and I know that, but the town doesn't. They still think you killed your uncle because he was going to fire you."

Ab's face reflected despair again. "I got this real strong feeling that I'm going to be in a cell the rest of my life."

"Not if you can get that memory of yours to help both of us out."

"I'll sure give it a try, Sheriff."

"You need to see me, just tell one of the deputies. Night or day, I'll be here."

"I appreciate that."

Matthews took the two empty tin coffee cups and carried them back up front.

TWO

ANNIE REYNOLDS WAS eating the last portion of her beef stew when the knock came. She took the extra time to carry her bowl to the sink and run a comb through her hair quickly. Then she glanced at the far end of the cottage, her work space. People just naturally figured that if you weren't pushing boulders up a steep hill, you weren't really working.

But candlemaking was tedious and intricate work. You had to get your tallow, the hard fat of cows, bears, sheep, deer, that you heated, at which point you began dipping the wick until you began to see a candle taking shape. But after you dipped it, you needed to let it cool, and then you dipped it again and so on and so on until the candle was large enough to burn for a time. One of the last things you did was add some spice or herbs to the tallow so that the candle would smell pleasant when you burned it. Burning animal fat wasn't exactly the sort of smell you wanted filling your house.

The man at the door was somebody she'd just assumed was long dead.

"My God," she said. "Paul."

"Howdy, Annie."

"You're actually alive."

He plucked at the skin of his cheek. "I seem to be."

"My God."

"You going to invite me in, Annie?"

"Oh—sure—yes—sorry."

She stood aside, let him come in. The suit was too large, the face too hollow, the skin too sallow, the eyes and voice dead.

He was ghost-gray. He seemed to creak and sway as he walked. He was twenty-two years old. He looked fifty.

He sat in the rocking chair. The way he sighed, he sighed with such force she worried he was going to die right on the spot.

"Where've you been the past four years?"

"South America."

"South America? Why?"

He looked up at her with eyes that suggested both sorrow and madness. "Had business there."

She just naturally accepted his explanation. But then she remembered when the doctor had Paul put in that terrible hospital where they'd beaten him and given him alternately scalding and freezing baths. They'd been trying to "cure" his bad habits, including all the fantasies he had. If you didn't know him, you'd think they were true.

But that wasn't the worst of it with Paul. Oh, no—sometimes the fantasies *were* true. She remembered the night he'd run home, still a boy, out of breath and sobbing, begging her to hide him, to not let the coppers take him. When he'd told her that he'd burned down the grocery store that wouldn't give them any more credit, she hadn't believed him. Poor Paul got so caught up in his lies that he believed them himself.

"You look like you don't believe me," he said.

"I'm trying to absorb all this, Paul. That's all. I thought you were dead—and here you are at my door. But you didn't really answer my question about what you were doing in South America."

He said, with a certain harshness, "Trying to forget what happened to our little sister."

"Oh, God, Paul."

"I take it serious even if you don't."

"I don't take it serious? Do you remember how I was after it happened? I was crazy with it, Paul. So don't tell me I didn't take it serious. If that's what you really think, then you walk the hell out of here right now. Do you understand me? Walk right out that door and never come back again." She shook her head. "Didn't take it serious? You should be ashamed of yourself for saying that. You really should. And you say it again, I'll run you out. I really will."

He didn't say anything for a long minute. He looked like a corpse in the chair. The circles under his eyes gave him the color of a ghoul. He smelled funny, too. Unclean.

"You look like you could use some food, Paul."

"I'd appreciate it."

"You have any money?"

"Not much."

She went over and started fixing him stew and bread. She said, "I didn't appreciate what you said just now."

"I'm sorry I said that."

He was not known to apologize much. His words touched her. She turned to him and said, "Thanks for saying that."

"I was just running off. You know how I am."

She went back to ladling out stew, buttering up some bread slices. "How long you been in town here?"

"Five days."

"Five days and you haven't seen me till now?"

"I've been busy."

"Doing what?"

"Just business. Taking care of a few things."

She brought his stew over. Set it on the small table. He got up uncertainly from the chair and made his way over. His face was drab gray in the lamplight.

He ate slowly and slurped while he ate. She just watched him. She was angry thinking about him showing up here. He'd have only one reason to come to town. That made her angry and that made her scared.

"When you planning on leaving?"

"When I'm done here."

"You gave me your word, Paul."

He raised his head. He had stew on his chin. He'd always been sloppy. He said, "I have a plan. I went to the inquest and everything." He laughed. "I even hid up in a tree the other night after they found Soames's body in his mansion."

"I don't want to hear it, Paul."

"That's 'cause you're scared to stick up for yourself."

She went over and sat down and tried not to think about her obvious reason for suspecting Paul of the worst.

"Soames is dead," she said.

He continued to eat.

"Did you kill him?"

He continued to eat.

"If the sheriff knew who we really are, he'd come after you, Paul."

When he finished, he used the faded cloth she'd set out as a napkin. He daubed at his mouth.

"You didn't answer my question, Paul."

"I don't intend to answer your question." He stared straight ahead when he spoke.

"I don't want anything to do with this."

"You might not have any choice."

"Maybe I should go to the sheriff."

He turned toward her for the first time. "You won't do that."

"Why?"

"You don't want to see me hang."

"There's an innocent man in jail."

"You don't have to worry about him."

"Why not?"

"Because now somebody else is dead. A Pinkerton man. That sheriff of yours'll know that Ab Soames didn't murder his uncle."

"Did you kill the Pinkerton man?"

He stood up. He smiled. His smile had always scared her.

"I was hoping you'd changed," she said.

"They need to pay for what they did."

"Did you kill two people over it, Paul? Isn't that enough?"

That chill, arrogant smile she despised. "No; no, big sister, it's not nearly enough. Not nearly enough."

He left quietly.

Just after dinner, Bryce Harlow sent his son Wayne to tell his two friends that he wanted to meet them at the hunting lodge at nine tonight. His son was seventeen, a star baseball player on the local team, and respected enough to make his case seriously. To each man, he said, "This is very important to my father. He wanted me to tell you that." The son was surprised to discover that the two men seemed even more upset than his father did. He was curious, of course, but he knew better than to try and get information out of them.

Successful businessmen sometimes got involved in unsavory matters and they were honorable enough to spare their families the details. Wayne had a friend whose father had made his original capital by selling rifles to Indians. The friend confessed this when they tried out some of the grape wine one night. He said this was the family scandal nobody knew about. In the morning he rode his bike over to the Harlow residence and begged Wayne not to ever breathe a word of what he'd said. The family would be shamed out of polite society, he said. And that was probably true.

In the West these days, the newly rich constantly revised their family histories. Judged by the kind of tall tales one heard in the fancy dining rooms of mansions, just about every rich man in the West had never done anything but serve his Lord, his country, and his family with great and honorable selflessness. You could see this even in the portraits these men had painted of themselves. By the time the wily artists got done with them, the men looked as handsome, noble, and eternal as the senators of ancient Rome, another bunch of cutthroats who passed themselves off as saintly and honorable.

Nine o'clock it was, young Wayne reported back to his father. The hunting lodge. The three of them.

THREE

T HE LODGE WAS actually a two-story white stucco house that had been built by a local architect who'd gone broke in one of the recent recessions. Harlow, Davies, Soames, and Nolan had split the cost four ways and bought it from the desperate man. If they'd been younger, they would've hauled out most of the furniture and set the place up for frolic. A lot of liquor, a lot of beer, and maybe a gal or two—saloon dancers who just might, if the price was right, be seduced by wine and money into taking off most of their clothes—and the kind of night that got talked about—and exaggerated—for years to come. The four men had, until ten years ago, been known to get on a train and go to Denver for a long weekend and do God only knows what in the more civilized saloons and bawdyhouses of that great metropolis. They always told their wives they were attending meetings of one of the innumerable civic clubs to which they belonged.

But that had changed ten years ago. And so when this house became available to them for so little money, they kept the place intact. They used the place as a starting point for hunting; for just relaxing when they wanted to be away from business or social engagements; or for playing some poker or euchre. There was very little liquor. The men were now in their fifties and hooch exacted a price they were no longer willing to pay. Who wanted to puke? Who wanted a hangover the next day? Who wanted to add the extra weight to an already bloated carcass? And who for God's sake, wanted wild women? Didn't Don Williams of First Presbyterian have to be treated for syphilis with everybody in town knowing about it? Who needed or wanted that kind of grief?

So the house became not so much a lodge as just a retreat for four men who shared a secret. Well, there had been four men, anyway. Now there were three.

They sat at the table they used for cards in the large downstairs room that was paneled and adorned with swords, citations, hats, handguns, and rifles used in the war. Of the original four, two had fought for the Gray, two for the Blue. There had been beery differences at first, but as with most of the men who headed west after the war, they tempered their differences and earnestly tried to see that the other men were just as sincere and honorable in their own beliefs. The only time there was still occasional trouble was when the alcohol level rose a mite high. Then the clamor came and old wounds bled once more.

The way the two men pushed their white business envelopes to the center of the table did look a bit like a card game. Envelopes with handwritten names on the front.

Hector Nolan, a white-haired gentleman with booze-brightened nose, kept his letter and read: "Mine says, 'Ten years ago on the night of September 12, you committed a terrible sin. You will pay twice for it. Once at my hands and once at God's. On September 14 at 11:00 P.M. at the old dock, I want the one of you who survives the next four nights to bring me an envelope with one hundred thousand dollars. Otherwise, a certain hotel maid whom you have already paid will write out a confession as to what she witnessed ten years ago. And that confession will be handed over to your local sheriff. This is serious business, as you will have learned by now from the death of your fellow criminal Gerald Soames.'"

Vernon Davies said, "How do we know this isn't just some opportunist?"

Bryce Harlow, a small and slender man with something of the church about him, said, "Maybe it's time we just give it all up."

Hector Nolan looked confused. Vernon Davies told him, "He means confess. Get it over with."

Nolan laughed. "Now there's a good idea. The three of us could die in prison together. We're old men, Bryce. Old men. Even if we got the minimum sentence, we'd die inside prison walls. I want to die with my wife and my children and my grandchildren at my bedside. I didn't work this hard all my life to die on some filthy prison cot with some hick convict watching me. I don't think that's the kind of death Vernon has in mind, either."

Harlow shook his head. "You're assuming we'll be found guilty."

"That's because we *are* guilty, Bryce. Or have you forgotten?"

"But look at who she was. My Lord, will anybody really care? Or will they even believe anybody who says it wasn't an accident?"

"That might work if the trial was here, Bryce," Davies said. "But remember, we won't be tried here where our friends and family connections would be able to help us."

"A change of venue," Harlow said, "that's not all that uncommon."

"Wouldn't work," Nolan said, taking one of his formidable Cuban cigars from the breast pocket of his suit coat. He almost always wore suits. The joke was he probably slept in them. The thing with the cigars was, by now his teeth were piss-yellow. The joke there was that Nolan could never get lost in the woods. All he had to do was smile and somebody'd find him. "You get a change of venue because there's prejudice in the community against the defendants. The people in that community don't know who we are. We were just on vacation there. No judge would grant a change of venue on those grounds."

"Listen to him," Harlow said. "Are you a lawyer?"

"No. But I've read enough about change of venue to know we wouldn't get one."

"This doesn't matter, none of it," Davies said.

Soames had been the leader of their group. There had never been an official vote or any kind of official recognition. He just naturally fell to the leadership role in that innate way that boys—and probably girls—always know without being told who is the leader in their group. He may be challenged but he'll quickly prove—usually with his fists—what most of the boys know instinctively, that he's the leader anyway. It would be left to the fools to challenge him. Davies spoke now as Soames would have, giving the definitive word on what was going to happen. "We don't have to worry about a change of venue because we're not going to the law. What we have to worry about is killing this bastard."

"Killing him? Vernon, you're talking about murder." Harlow looked sick, as if he'd heard something that had defiled his most basic principles. "We're not killers."

"We're not killers because we never had to be," Davies said, "till now."

"Gosh, Vernon," Nolan said, "killing somebody. I don't know. I was thinking of hiring some local fellas to go with us to the dock that night and—" He glanced at Harlow, then back to Davies. "But you're talking about murder."

"You're forgetting something here, you two," Davies said.

"What's that?" Harlow said.

"He murdered Gerry Soames. Cold-blooded murder."

"That's right," Nolan said. He glanced at Harlow again. "I think Vernon's got a good point there."

This was how it had usually gone when Soames presided over the group. He put something forth and the others would skittishly discuss it because Soames was a tough man and he did things that walked just on the edge of being legal. He'd always been amused by how, one by one, they'd come to his side. And this was always the pattern. You snared Nolan first. And then Nolan went to work on Harlow. Harlow was never easy—he liked to pretend that he lived by a much higher standard of moral preferences than did his more cynical friends—but he always gave in because what Soames inevitably argued for was their survival as a group and as individuals. Not even the pious Harlow could ultimately vote against that.

"You're overlooking something," Harlow said.

"What's that?"

"The way he wrote this letter, it sounds like he plans to leave only one of us alive."

"Braggadocio," Davies said. "Trying to scare us."

"He killed Gerry Soames, didn't he?" Harlow said.

"That doesn't mean he can kill *us*," Davies said. "I'm taking a gun with me everywhere I go. I'm not going out at night. And I've given everybody in my house the word not to let anybody in, no matter who they are. Day or night. Until this is settled."

"He also killed a Pinkerton man," Harlow said. "That took some doing. Pinkerton men are generally pretty tough customers."

Davies said, "C'mon now, Harlow. Climb down off that damned high horse of yours and throw in with us. There's only one way to deal with this fellow and you know it. Either he gets it or we do."

"I wasn't aware I was *on* a high horse, Vernon. It's

just that I don't seem to have the killer instinct you two do. Killing somebody's a pretty terrible thing to do."

"Yes, it is," Davies said, "and if we hadn't already killed somebody we wouldn't be in this fix."

"Now that's not fair to any of us," Harlow said. "That was a very different circumstance."

"Is that how you live with yourself?" Davies smirked. "Telling yourself that it was a different circumstance? That's what I meant by your high horse. At least admit to yourself what we did."

"I didn't start it, if you'll remember."

"No, Harlow, but you sure didn't run away when it got going, either, did you?"

"C'mon," Nolan said. "This is just what he wants. For us to start tearing each other down this way."

"I'm afraid what he wants, Nolan," Davies said, "is one hundred thousand dollars."

"He thinks we're a lot richer than we are," Nolan said. "Divided three ways—"

Davies liked to think what he saw on Nolan's face was a sudden recognition bordering on the religious. Fine and dandy to talk about killing or not killing their blackmailer. That was in the abstract. Money was not in the abstract. Divide one hundred thousand dollars three ways and you had a whopping amount of money for men who'd been cash-strapped by the present recession that was sprawling across the land like an invading army.

"I don't think I could raise my end of that without doing some pretty fast dancing," Harlow said. "I'm overextended up to here. And the vet says that a lot of my cattle picked up some kind of infection over the last three weeks. I don't know where *that's* going. What if it keeps spreading through the herd and the vet can't do anything about it? I've got to make some pretty good money this fall or I'm in a lot of trouble."

"My problem with it is what happens if he comes back on us," Nolan said. "That's what I'm worried about." He turned to Harlow. "That's where I think Vernon's right. We need to get rid of this fella once and for all."

"You kill any men in the war?" Harlow asked.

"Couple, I guess. Maybe three. Why?" Nolan said.

"You kill 'em up close?"

"Not real close."

"What's your point, Harlow?" Davies said.

"That we're not cold-blooded murderers. That's my point." Harlow touched his chin as if considering a thought. "I killed four men in the war. I would've killed five, but *him* I had to kill up close and I couldn't do it. I shot him in the leg and the shoulder. But I couldn't take his life. And you know why? Because I saw his face and saw that he was probably just like me. Scared and confused about the whole thing and just wanting to get back home to his family. That's how most of us were in the war. We didn't want to be there and we didn't want to kill people. But they forced us to."

"And that's supposed to mean what exactly?" Davies said. "This blackmailing bastard is sure forcing us to kill him."

"Not really. We have options."

"I'm not turning myself in," Nolan said. "If that's one of your so-called options, you can forget about it."

"I'm thinking of reasoning with him," Harlow said.

Davies laughed out loud. "I'm sorry, Harlow. I don't mean to make fun of you. I know you believe all that Sunday school bullshit you spout all the time. But this mess is way beyond Sunday school rules. He's killed two men, so we know he's ruthless. He's threatened to kill two of us, so we know he's dangerous. And he's demanding a sum of money we can't afford."

"And," Nolan said for the second time, "there's nothing to stop him from coming back and back again. You know how these people operate. He'll go out and spend the money and then in six months or a year he'll be back at the trough for another feeding. I don't know if I'm a cold-blooded killer or not—I worked in supplies during the war and that didn't give me much of a chance for combat—but I'll tell you one thing, Harlow. I'm willing to *find out* if I'm a cold-blooded killer or not. You put a gun in my hand and face me off with him and I've got a hunch I could do the job. All I'd have to remember are the things Vernon here mentioned tonight. We've got a right to protect ourselves, don't we? And this is the only way I can see us doing it."

"Then it's decided?" Davies said.

Harlow shook his head. "I haven't decided yet." He hesitated. "Say for the sake of argument I went along with this, Davies. When would we kill him?"

"When we meet him to hand over the money. At the dock."

"What if he sends somebody else?"

"Then we threaten to kill that somebody else until he tells us where the blackmailer can be found."

"What if the blackmailer's hiding somewhere and as soon as his cohort gets the money, he opens fire on us?"

" 'Us.' " Nolan smiled. "Remember, he said that only one of us was going to be alive by then."

"We'll be alive," Davies said with self-conscious bluster. "You don't have to worry about that." Then: "There's a shallow stand of pines up at the top of the hill behind the old dock. That's the only place he can hide. And one of us'll be hiding there, too."

"One of us?" Harlow said.

"Sure. We'll be covered in case he tries something like that. Fine for him to put a man up there. We'll have one up there, too."

"This could all come apart so easy," Harlow said. His face was shiny with sweat. He licked dry lips.

"You're scared," Davies said, "and that's fine. I'm scared, too, and so is Nolan. But that's the only thing that can hurt us—fear. If we can get around that, then he's all done. There're three of us, this is our town, and he's killed two men in the way they hang you for. You say we're cold-blooded, Harlow. But we're not. He's the one who's cold-blooded. He's the one we need to stop."

"What about Reed Matthews?" Harlow said. "He's not stupid. He knows what goes on around here. What if he finds out?"

"We'll deal with him if and when we need to," Davies said. He paused and then his expression softened. "You know what's funny here? You and me, Bryce Harlow and Vernon Davies. The best of friends since we met a long time ago. And the same with Hector, here. Best of friends. We're only missing poor Gerry Soames to make a quorum."

"I don't see anything funny in that," Harlow said.

"Bryce — what's funny is that we're talking like we're enemies. He's dividing us. He's making us forget that we're friends. That we trust each other. That we want to help each other. Isn't that how it's always been between us? One of us gets in trouble and the others pitch in and help out. I wouldn't have made the money I have without you boys helping me out from time to time. And the same goes for you. I've helped both of you two plenty of times, too."

"He's right, Bryce," Nolan said.

"Now we're in a place where we need to help each other again is all I'm saying," Davies said. "The difference is that this time it's not just our money, it's our lives. This sonofabitch is crazy. He wants vengeance. He wants money, sure. But anybody who'd kill Gerry Soames and the Pinkerton man — he wants vengeance most of all. So if we don't stand together on this, we don't have a chance. Because he'll keep coming at us and coming at us. And he's not going to stop."

A troubled silence. Davies and Nolan stared at Harlow. Harlow looked self-conscious. He frowned and bit his lip and shook his head, all in response to the thoughts he was having. It was obvious that he still didn't like Davies's plan. But it was equally obvious that at this point there didn't seem to be any alternative.

"I suppose you're right," Harlow said quietly.

Davies and Nolan knew not to celebrate. Not to tell him that he was doing the right thing. Not to tell him that he was finally seeing reality.

All Davies said was: "I'll kill him when the time comes. I won't ask either of you to do that."

"At the dock?" Nolan said.

"At the dock and at the time we hand him the money."

"How about the man we put up on the hill?" Nolan said. "Who'll that be?"

"I'll let you two decide. None of us here is a great shot. So it comes down to nerve and will. We put a man up there in the woods and he has to have the balls to kill somebody—back-shoot him if necessary—when the time comes."

"What if it's the blackmailer on the hill and his cohort on the dock?" Harlow said. "You still kill the one on the dock?"

"Absolutely. At that point he'll be just as dangerous as the blackmailer. He'll most likely know everything the blackmailer knows. Which means that he could turn right around and start blackmailing us himself."

But Harlow wasn't quitting. Even though he was going along with everything, he clearly wanted it known that there were all kinds of risks involved. "What if the blackmailer told somebody else about us? Somebody besides his cohort."

"What if the moon falls down?" Davies said. His voice was getting tight again. He forced himself to speak in a friendlier way. "Look, we're not professionals. We're just trying to save our asses from prison. If we start worrying about every possible contingency—"

"He's right, Bryce," Nolan said. "We'll never get *any*thing done if we start worrying it all to death."

Harlow sighed. "I guess you're right. I guess I do have a tendency to worry about things too much."

"Right now we have one enemy," Davies said. "And that's the blackmailer. We talk about a cohort of his, but we don't even know if he *has* a cohort. Maybe he's doing the whole shebang. We'll just have to see how it plays out. There's nothing else we can do."

Hector Nolan yawned. "Then it's settled?"

Davies smiled affectionately. "Only Hector could yawn while we're talking about life and death."

Ten minutes later, they were each on their horses and headed back to town.

By the time the three men left the lodge, Karen Davies was so cold that her entire body was shivering. Knowing that her father would never tell her what he was so worried about lately, she'd decided to follow him. The first surprise was that he went to the hunting lodge. The second surprise was that Nolan and Harlow were there. Whatever was going on must be highly secret, she realized as she crouched near the windows on the northern wall of the place. And it must involve "his group," as he always described them.

The fall night had become a rival to a bitter November night. At least as far as temperature and wind velocity were concerned. She wished she'd worn her long underwear. Her butternuts, sweater, and lined work jacket just weren't enough. She'd also have been smart to bring along carmuffs. Thank God she wore lined gloves. Even so, her knuckles were numb with the cold.

She had no idea what they were talking about at first.

She wished she had heard everything. Something had happened ten years ago that involved them. That was all. And that would never become any clearer, either. Not tonight, anyway.

What *was* clear was that their secret—whatever it was—had gotten Gerry Soames murdered. And shortly after him, the Pinkerton man.

But bad as those revelations had been, what stunned her the most was the talk of the men going to prison. She was strictly selfish. Her only concern was her father. He had become so heavy, so slow physically, and so forgetful that she couldn't imagine him surviving even a week in prison. Even a girl raised to be a genteel lady knew about prison life. Or some of it, anyway. She was always being asked to sign petitions that would authorize investigations into the treatment of the convicts. She was, in her father's phrase, a "helping hand." He always spoke those words with amused contempt.

"Hell," he'd said, "why should a man in prison expect to get treated like a king?"

"I don't expect him to be treated like a king, Dad. But I don't expect him to be tortured, either. Or starved to death. Or beaten up or killed by the prison guards."

"You're just like your mother. She was always on me about women getting the vote. I s'pose that'll be the next thing with you. Women voting."

"It already is, Dad. I'm marching in a big rally in Denver next month."

At this point he usually smiled and said: "Well, when the coppers arrest you, use a false name, will you? I don't want the Davies name being tied up with numbskull causes like that one."

But Dad wasn't smiling about anything these days. Whatever he and the others had done had turned their minds to committing murder. Three respectable men of retirement age, their financial capital blighted by bad weather, the recession, and bank failures—resorting to discussing murder.

FOUR

SHE TOOK A shortcut through the woods. There was enough moonlight and enough path for her horse to move comfortably and quickly, despite the slapping of a few pine branches and a couple of narrowing passages where she had to slow the animal. She wanted to get home before her father did. She didn't want him wondering where she'd gone tonight. She went out so seldom that he'd get curious for sure.

Carmella, the maid, was in her room off the kitchen, sleeping, when Karen came home. She snored with the ferocity of a drunken sailor. She'd fixed up very nicely what had been a large storage room.

When her father came in, Karen was sitting in front of the fireplace wrapped in a shawl, a steaming cup of coffee in one hand and a copy of *The Return of the Native* by Thomas Hardy in the other. Her library discussion group had decided to read the Hardy now that it was available in an inexpensive reprint edition.

"You look nice and comfy," her father said, kissing her on the forehead. He stood in front of the fire warming his backside, rubbing his hands. "Played cards a lot longer than I wanted to tonight."

She placed her bookmark against the page she was reading and then closed the novel. Her impulse was to tell her father that she knew he was in trouble and to please let her help him. She had to fight against that impulse because she knew that he would first be hurt and then furious if he knew she'd followed him. He was one of those men—one of the few, in her limited experience—who resented mothering. Took away from his sense of himself as an independent, grown-up, and capable man. He didn't need any skirt chasing after him to help him out of trouble.

But she saw in the tired eyes and the drawn mouth and the heavy slump of the shoulders a man who knew—even if he wouldn't admit it to himself and he damned well wouldn't—that he was up against something he wasn't sure he could conquer. He was used to conquering, all the successful men in the West were. You kicked, slugged, bit, bribed, stomped a problem until you'd conquered it, and then went on to the next problem. But he was an old man and his days of conquest were over. This recession had left him more financially—and thus mentally and spiritually—vulnerable than he'd been since the days before he'd made his first fortune.

"You look cold, honey," he said. "You feeling all right?"

"Just a chill."

He smiled. "You and your chills. I remember the first time we ever took you sledding. I don't think you got warm for at least a week."

The fondness of his tone moved her. She realized how much he loved her and realized how much she loved him. And now she was terrified for him. Even though she didn't know all the details, she knew that he needed help of some kind. She'd have gone right to Reed Matthews if her father hadn't talked about prison earlier tonight. And it wasn't just prison. It was also the prospect of one of the three men — Dad, Harlow, Nolan — being murdered. No, this wasn't something Dad could handle at all by himself.

He coughed. He had a tendency to get the croup. A chill, foggy, damp night like this one wasn't good for him. She said, "How does hot tea sound?" Much as he was against mothering, he was one of those men who would never think of preparing tea, coffee, cider, or anything else for himself. Well, with one exception: He would, when the time was right, fix a drink for himself. A good stiff one. That was the extent of waiting on himself. That's what wives and daughters were for. And maids. Waiting on men.

When she returned with his tea, she found him in a comfortable chair angled toward the fireplace. He was dozing, exhausted. She thought about not waking him but if he slept at this angle much longer, he'd get a crick in his neck. She touched his hand. He woke, as he usually woke, startled and gasping around for some unseen enemy.

"It's all right, Dad," she soothed, touching her slender hand to his brawny one. "Everything's fine."

He accepted the tea, sat up straight in the chair. "You're too good to me."

"I think you've got that the other way around."

She went over and sat again by the fire. In times past, her mother would have sat in a third chair. Karen had loved to hear them talk about adult things. She had always had the sense that no matter how old she got she would never have their knowledge or wisdom about the world. Only lately had she changed her mind. Her father was now facing one of the worst—if not *the* worst—confrontations of his life, and all he could do was talk about murdering somebody, which was hardly a solution. She wanted to say to him, *You want to kill a man so you can avoid going to jail? Don't you see how ridiculous that is? If you kill this man and they catch you, you'll not only go to jail, they'll hang you for premeditated murder.* Growing up meant more than a simple loss of innocence; it meant realizing that nobody had easy answers for anything.

They talked. Or rather, he talked. Whenever he was melancholy, he talked about the old days. He told the same stories over and over. He took solace from being once again the young man who'd seen how to economize the short-haul railroad business—even though people had laughed at his ideas at first. The young man who had his own business by age twenty-four. The young man whom one newspaper had called "The Man with the Midas Touch." The cliché of it didn't bother him at all. He still had that newspaper clipping, now a deep faded brown, framed and hanging in his den.

She listened. She knew when she was expected to marvel aloud at his accomplishments. This was all as formal as a waltz, this dance of nostalgia they did. But what she was really doing was trying to figure out a way to help her father. He was too frightened and too old to think clearly. His friends were no help, either. Bryce Harlow was sensible enough to argue against murder, but he had no alternative plan. Nolan, as usual, had ended up going along with her father, as he almost always did.

And then it was bedtime.

She let her father go upstairs first. She cleaned up the kitchen—she was embarrassed to leave a mess for the maid—and went around turning down the lamps. It was while she was at the front window, peering out at the faded gold light of the street lamp, that she saw somebody slip behind the wide oak tree directly across the street.

Him.

She knew it instantly. Had no doubt.

Him.

It was funny, her first impulse upon seeing him duck behind the tree after realizing that she'd seen him—her first impulse was to get her own gun and kill him. She didn't give a damn that he wanted money. What she cared about was that he was destroying the last few years of her father's life. For that, he deserved to die.

But the impulse faded and she let the curtain drop

back into place. No, she would have to take care of him in some other way. But how?

That single thought stayed with her as she combed her hair out, as she washed her face and hands, as she slipped into her nightshirt, and as she plumped the pillow so she'd have a comfortable position for her reading.

Yet she had a difficult time reading because all she could think of was him. She wondered if he was still out there. Still watching the house.

And then for the first time, she wondered *why* he was watching the house. What good would it do him? What could he possibly learn from watching the house? All she could think of was that he was deriving some kind of personal pleasure from this. That this was more than about blackmail and money. That this was terror, intimidating three old men and watching them crumble.

But what was she going to do about it? What *could* she do about it?

FIVE

REED MATTHEWS WOKE up—much against his will—just before midnight. Somebody pounding on his door made further sleep impossible.

He slept in the bottom of his long underwear, no shirt except in the worst of the winter months. He jerked on jeans. He grabbed his Colt and went to answer the knock.

Roy Fuller stood there, blood snaking down his face from some kind of cut on his head. He was a dapper little fellow, dressed in a suit and cravat even at this hour. Even now, even bloodied this way, he was dapper.

He said, "Somebody broke into the office and slugged me."

"Roy, I hate like hell to say this," Matthews said, trying to keep from sounding irritated. "But isn't this something that Harold could handle down at my office? Harold is an awfully good man."

"I'm sorry," Roy said, his small, refined face reflecting his own irritation. "But since this involves the office of my employer—and one of the most important citizens of this entire valley—and since it's well known that you and Karen are good friends—I thought I'd come straight here."

Roy Fuller was Vernon Davies's accountant. Davies had an office in town, the central point for all of his business interests.

"Here?" Matthews looked behind him at the messy cottage. He was not a neat and tidy man. In fact, he distrusted neat and tidy men. He had never met a neat and tidy man he'd liked. Never. "This isn't a place where I meet folks."

"Well, then, why don't you put on a shirt and we can stand out here and I can tell you about it."

Matthews sighed. "All right. Wait here. But you sure you don't want to go down to the office and talk to Harold?"

"I doubt that's what Mr. Davies would want me to do. When *he* deals with people, he always deals with the top man and nobody less."

"I see. All right, then. Wait here."

"It was about twenty minutes ago."

"You were at the office twenty minutes ago? Why?"

"I was working, Sheriff. Why else would I be there?"

"I just meant, isn't it kind of late to be working?"

"Not if you're conscientious. Not when there's so much work to do that you can't sleep for worrying about it. Not when your wife tells you that you may as well just get up and go to the office because you're driving her crazy with all your tossing and turning in bed."

"I see. So you're working. And then what?"

"Well—and Mr. Davies certainly won't be happy to hear this—I must've left the door unlocked because he got in with no problem. And snuck up behind me without hearing him."

"Did he say anything before he knocked you out?"

"He certainly did. Quite a mouthful, in fact. He said he was just itching to kill somebody—and that's exactly how he put it, too, 'itching to kill somebody'—and that it might as well be me." He made a sour little face. "I frankly thought that kind of thing was behind us now that the West is civilized."

"Parts of it are civilized. Not all of it. Not yet."

Fuller touched the top of his head and retrieved fingers sticky and red with blood. "Well, I guess my poor head can testify to that fact, now, can't it, Sheriff?"

"He wanted money?"

"Yes. And he wouldn't believe me when I told him we didn't keep much on hand. A hundred or so at most. Just about every transaction is done with a check. There's no reason to keep a lot of cash on hand. It may as well be in the bank. But he didn't believe me. I gave him the one hundred thirty-four dollars from the cash box and nine dollars of my own. But that wasn't good enough. That's why he took the files, I guess. He must've thought I was hiding cash in them. Which, of course, I wasn't. Why would I hide money in files?"

"What kind of files?"

"Ordinary client files. Transactions, debits and credits, things like that. A recession like this, we have to make a special effort to get people to pay their bills. That's why I have so much work to do. Just trying to get people to give us our money. How can we be expected to pay our bills if nobody pays us? I think that's a pretty reasonable attitude. As does Mr. Davies."

"How many files were there?"

"Twenty or so."

"And he just walked off with them?"

"Yes — right after he slugged me. And he seemed to take great pleasure in slugging me, I might add. He laughed when he did it."

"Well, what I'd like you to do now is go to my office and tell Harold about this. Give him a description of the man. He'll start looking for him right away."

"I take it you're going back to bed?"

"I'd say that's pretty much my own business, Mr. Fuller."

"You're not going to help Harold look for this bastard?"

"Harold's a good man, the way I said."

Fuller craned his neck, looked beyond. "So then you *are* going back to bed?"

"Yes, Mr. Fuller; yes, I am going back to bed. I put in a long day, I'm tired, and I'm now going back to bed."

"While Harold and I are out searching for this man, you'll be sleeping?"

"You're going with Harold?"

"Well, of course. It's my duty to protect Davies's interests. That includes his files. I will definitely be accompanying Harold."

Lucky Harold, Matthews thought. "Well, good night, then, Mr. Fuller."

"I'll see that everybody in town knows that you went back to bed. You hold an elective office, don't forget."

"Gosh, Mr. Fuller, I'd forgotten all about that until you reminded me just now. I appreciate you mentioning it. Good night, Mr. Fuller."

He went back inside, fighting the impulse to slam the door. Instead, he closed it gently. He was asleep in four minutes.

•

Ab Soames imagined it this way: He stood at the front of a long, dark hallway at the end of which, backlit in white, stood the silhouette of the man he'd seen running from his uncle's den. The silhouetted man was the killer. This proved to Ab that no matter how tangled up his memory got, *he* wasn't the killer. Sometimes in his drunkenness, Ab would think about killing somebody. Then he'd wake up in the middle of the night, terrified that he'd actually done just that. He'd force himself back to sleep, the only way he could escape his fantasy of killing someone—if it *had* been a fantasy. This mixture of reality and unreality was the worst part of drinking, at least for Ab. Puking, peeing all over himself, falling down, even shitting all over himself—all these rolled together was nothing compared to waking up and not knowing what you'd done the night before. God knows all the terrible things you *could* have done. But *had* he done them?

The cells were empty but for him tonight. Not even a drunk. So there wasn't much else to do except try and figure out who he'd seen rushing from his uncle's den.

This was different from his other memory losses. If he couldn't figure this one out, he might well end up on the business end of a noose.

He stared down the dark tunnel of his mind at the silhouette. The figure was so distant, Soames couldn't even get an impression of how big the man was. Or even if it *was* a man for sure. The frame of the door should have given him a reference of scale—how tall, how wide the silhouette was—but somehow it didn't.

In fact, the only thing Soames got out of his troubles tonight was one hell of a headache.

He closed his eyes and thought of fishing. During his stretches of sobriety, fishing comforted him. Especially when he went alone. Standing out in the water a quarter mile beneath a dam was especially fun. He forgot about what a failure he was and how much he hated himself. That was a funny thing to do, to despise yourself the way he did. In his case there were a lot of other people happy to hate him. He didn't need any help. But when he was fishing . . .

So there he was on a fine late-summer day, standing in the middle of the river and all of a sudden—

All of a sudden he was back at the front of that long, dark hallway again. The figure moved. Not much. Just sort of angled to the left. But in doing so made itself *familiar* in some way it hadn't been before.

There was something about it now. . . .

Ab Soames forgot all about fishing and concentrated on standing at the front of that hallway, closely observing that damned silhouette, hoping it would move itself again . . . and become even *more* familiar to him . . .

•   •   •

Harold Lincoln said, "Well, he didn't make much of a mess."

Roy Fuller said, tartly, of course, "Is that supposed to make me feel better?"

Friendly Sheepdog Harold said to Ill-Tempered Pekingese Roy, "Look, Roy, I know you wish Sheriff Matthews would've handled this himself. But it is late and the fella does deserve his sleep and I'll be the first to admit that I'm not up to par as a lawman where he's concerned, but this is a pretty open-and-shut case and one I feel I can handle well enough right now to turn over to Sheriff Matthews in the morning. All I said was that the robber didn't make much of a mess. Sometimes those fellows like to bust stuff up to show you how tough they are and everything. But this fella just seemed to want the money and nothing else. And I can't figure out for the life of me why you'd go and get all thundered up about me making a harmless little remark like that." He swept a hand across the small office. "He didn't, in fact, make much of a mess. That's all I said."

Roy Fuller looked as if he might still have a little acid in him. But then he seemed to think it over. "I apologize, Deputy. I'm tired. I'm frustrated. And my head hurts. Tomorrow morning, Mr. Davies is going to give me a verbal thrashing that I'll remember the rest of my life."

"It wasn't your fault you got robbed."

"No, but it was my fault that I left the door unlocked."

"I guess you forgot to tell me that."

"Yes, I guess I did. But now you can see why I'm so irritable."

Gosh, I thought you were always this way, Harold Lincoln wanted to say. But he knew better, him being a lowly night deputy and Fuller here being an accountant with a high school degree and all. "Why don't you show me how it happened, Mr. Fuller?"

"Show you?"

Harold Lincoln nodded. Because of the rain they'd been having, he wore his huge white Stetson, the one his kids loved to make fun of. When he nodded like he did just now, the Stetson sloped downward, damned near covering his eyes. That was the part his kids liked best. They loved making fun of their pop, but not half as much as their pop loved being made fun *of*. Hearing them giggle was his favorite sound in all the world.

"I don't see how that could help."

"If you don't do it for me, Sheriff Matthews'll have you do it for him."

"Since when is this a part of taking care of a robbery?"

"Sheriff Matthews has taken a lot of courses. And that's the way they teach you to do it."

"What courses?"

"State capital. They've got a police school there."

"A police school," Fuller said. "Just another excuse for town and county employees to take even more time off work if you ask me. I'm sorry to say that, but that's the way I feel about things of that sort."

"So why don't you sit at your desk over there and I'll pretend to be the robber and you pretend to be working."

Roy Fuller sighed with deep disgust. "I really need my sleep, Deputy. This is such a waste of time."

"Couple minutes is all it'll take, Mr. Fuller. Not any longer than that."

It was like a child's game, way it turned out. Fuller pretending to be working, Lincoln acting like the robber.

Fuller sighed a lot. Lincoln wrote down several things in the back-pocket notebook Matthews had taught him to carry.

"So he came in here," Lincoln said.

"Where else would he come in?" Fuller said. "It's the only door into the office."

"I'll try to keep my thoughts to myself, Mr. Fuller. I just seem to make you mad when I think out loud."

"I'm just tired, is all. Tired and scared I'll lose my job because I was so damned stupid tonight when I left that door open. The very door we're talking about right this minute, in fact."

Harold Lincoln was true to his word. He did not think aloud even one more time. He wrote six more things down in his notebook. Roy Fuller kept right on sighing. If they had a sighing contest at the county fair this fall, Harold Lincoln knew who'd win.

Karen Davies woke up around two, lying there wide awake until four, at which point she went downstairs to her father's den.

She spent half an hour going through desk drawers and filing cabinets. She found what she wanted in a simple white envelope in the bottom of the lowest of his desk drawers, hidden away inside a book on insurance. Her search was thorough so when she saw the tip of the envelope sticking up in the insurance guide, she immediately lifted it out and looked at it.

She couldn't be sure that this was the source of her father's trouble, but she was pretty sure. Why else would he hide it away like this? And the newspaper clipping was from ten years ago, the time her father seemed to start aging so rapidly. All this could be a complete coincidence. She had to keep that in mind. The story could pertain to some friend of his — maybe the victim's father was a friend of his — and as for the aging . . . well, he had to start aging sometime, didn't he? Maybe ten years ago was just the time his body started giving out on him.

But she didn't think so.

Once she'd read the newspaper story three times, she started looking again for corroborative material. Anything. Letters, maps, more clippings. She remembered the time he'd gone on that vacation with "his group." She thought of all the changes since then. Each of the men had become an old man since. But when they'd embarked on that week-long hunting and fishing vacation, they'd still been strong, virile, and feisty. With the exception of Bryce Harlow, they still tended to raise hell every once in a while like young men. Dad had still been known to punch people from time to time. No more. That all ended . . . ten years ago.

She found nothing else.

She replaced everything except the clipping, which she took back upstairs to her room. She lay on the bed. Dawn had always frightened her. Something about the transition to day. Whenever the world ended, it would end at dawn, she'd always sensed. Night protected; night hid the worst of your personal secrets. But dawn meant daylight and daylight meant all the smiling, lying faces that used sweet words to mask treachery. Not big treachery. Just gossip. Just the smiting of other souls with words. Just the grand deception, lies being passed from human to human, and exaggerated along the way, so that even the original lies got distorted way out of proportion. Just the condescension people piled upon "old maids," especially those who came from some money.

She tried to forget about the clipping and sleep. But couldn't. What she really should do was confront Dad with it. Get this all out in the open. Tell him that she knew his plans and was going to stop him. She played this little drama over in her head several times. But even as much as she practiced it, she knew she'd never be able to brace her father that way. Not so much because of the secret he was hiding, but because such a confrontation would appear to him the ultimate sign of disrespect. Even though all she was trying to do was help him.

She started feeling badly about herself. Wasn't she an adult? Wasn't her grown-up responsibility, therefore, to stop her father before he won himself a place on the gallows? Shouldn't she be willing to put her own anxiety aside and tell him she was doing this for his sake and that if he didn't promise to drop his plans, she'd tell Reed Matthews what was going on?

And then she realized that maybe there was a simpler way around this whole blackmail thing. Nobody knew that she knew what was going on with the demand for money and the threat of exposure. What if she dealt with the blackmailer herself, and didn't tell her father anything about it? If she did turn to Reed Matthews, her father would likely die in prison. It she didn't, he'd likely kill the blackmailer and end up hanging.

But what if *she* killed the blackmailer? He had to be the man she'd seen lurking around the house. What if she hid across the street until he came to watch their house? And what if she followed him and killed him? She could wait until her father and Bryce Harlow and Hector Nolan were out somewhere with a public alibi. And then she could kill him. . . .

Who would suspect an old maid of such a thing? People would laugh if you even brought it up.

The idea was so ridiculous that the first thing she did was smile. But eventually the smile faded and the idea didn't seem so ridiculous anymore.

She finally went to sleep with the idea at least half-serious in her mind. Nobody would ever suspect her. Not even her father.

SIX

Dear Sheriff Matthews—

*In the future please see that I get every chance
possible to work with Mr. Roy Fuller. He is a pure
pleasure. You'll find my robbery report on your
desk also.*

*Sincerely,
Harold Lincoln*

The tone of the note was typical Harold. He loved quiet
sarcasm. Reed Matthews, sitting at his desk as the morning's sunbeams shot through the window turning otherwise invisible air into thick and churning gold motes of
dust, smiled and started in on the robbery report. Nothing droll there. Harold knew when to joke and when to
be strictly professional. Harold and Matthews both thought

it was strange that a robber would hold up a business office. Business offices generally didn't have much cash
on hand. But then, as Harold conjectured in his report,
the culprit was probably drunk, probably desperate, and
probably couldn't find anyplace else with lights burning
except the saloons. And trying to rob a saloon was a sui-
cide mission. You didn't have to worry about the bar-
tender pulling up a sawed-off from beneath the bar. By
that time you'd already be dead. The drunkards
would've taken care of you by then, punching, kicking,
and shooting you for good measure. They didn't like
their drinking interrupted.

So the robber settled for what he could find and what
he found was the business office of Vernon Davies.
Matthews got up and put the report on the desk of his
best day deputy, Rafferty. This was his kind of job.
Matthews had two murders to worry about.

Now that he'd gone through all the reports from last
night, he poured out two cups of coffee and went back to
the cells.

Ab Soames was sleeping. Matthews called his name
several times. Soames responded slowly, groggily. Then
suddenly realizing where he was and who was calling
him, he sat up straight, rubbed his face, and jumped to
his feet. He went to the slot in the cell door and took the
two cups from Matthews. Matthews then let himself in,
locking the door behind him.

"You look pretty tired, Sheriff."

"So do you."

Soames sipped coffee, nodded. "I was awake for a

long time. Workin' on tryin' to remember who I saw runnin' from my uncle's den."

"You come up with anything?"

"Not yet. I mean, nothin' like a face or a name. But it's funny."

"What is?"

"I'm gettin' this *feeling*."

"What kind of feeling?"

"That I know him."

"You mean the man you saw running away?"

"Yeah. That I know him pretty good, in fact."

The lawman sighed. "You're drivin' me crazy, Ab. You just gotta figure this out. For everybody's sake."

Ab frowned. He looked wasted and worn and sad. "I know I do, Sheriff. I just hope I can do it is all. I sure do hope I can do it."

"We recently got a vaudeville in Denver," Dennis McCabe said. He was a stout Pinkerton man who dressed like a drummer. "Maybe you two could try out for that."

Matthews and Rafferty had been telling McCabe jokes after they'd been seated in the café. He hadn't found them very funny.

After their coffee came, McCabe said, "Anything new on our man?"

"Not so far. We got the body shipped back yesterday. And as I said in my wire, I'm giving you all the daily reports I write."

"You keep daily reports?"

"Have to. Otherwise, when you get in court, there's a good chance that defense lawyers'll make a fool of you.

And I don't need any help looking like a fool. You say such-and-such and they say no, you couldn't possibly have done that on the date you said. So I have my daily reports to back me up."

"Smart man."

"Not smart. Vain. Even if I *am* a fool, I don't enjoy looking like one."

"I'm going to do a little looking around myself."

"Figured you would. And that's fine with me. Sooner we figure out what's going on here, the happier I'll be. Two murders in such a short time—the town council'll be wanting to toss my ass out of here if I don't come up with something soon. You know how they get. Afraid the town'll get the same reputation it had back in the boom-town days. And two murders do make you sit up and take notice."

"You think they're connected?"

"I'm pretty sure they are." Matthews sipped his coffee and said, "Wait a minute. Why wouldn't they be connected?"

"Why would they be?"

"Well, Gerald Soames gets killed. Gerald Soames is a friend of Vernon Davies. Davies was the one who hired your agency. A small town like this, it sure seems suspicious if nothing else."

"I guess you're probably right," the Pinkerton man said. "I have an appointment with Davies in an hour. I'm hoping he can tell me what Dwight finds out."

"Where's your appointment?"

"His house. I could use some help with directions."

"No trouble there." Matthews finished his coffee. "You'll earn your money with Davies."

"Is he a tough guy?"

"He thinks he is." Matthews laughed. "Those're the worst kind."

That afternoon, after going back to the Soames place and talking again to the butler and the maid, Matthews took the river road back to the heart of town, and it was there he saw the stranger on Annie Reynolds's doorstep. He wasn't jealous. There'd been a time in the relationship when he'd thought that Annie and he might actually become lovers. But she wasn't the sort to settle down with one man, and so they'd just become friends. She liked the reflected glory of knowing the sheriff, and he liked having somewhere to go besides a saloon or his empty cottage.

Still, the man at her door gave Matthews a start. This was the man he'd seen in the back of the courtroom at the inquest. Who was he, anyway? Maybe Annie had got herself a new beau from a nearby town. Or maybe this was an old suitor. Or maybe this was just somebody from that past of hers, the one she never quite talked about.

The door opened. He glimpsed Annie but she didn't see him. The man went inside. The door closed.

He thought about the stranger all the way back to the office. But just as soon as he was seated behind his desk, Mayor Ken Thomas's voice filled the front part of the building. He had a voice that irritated Matthews, one of those loud, insistent voices that had a disagreeable undertone even when it tried to sound friendly. He was one of those men who listened to you until you said something he could pounce on. He kept getting reelected for one reason: His negative attitude and braying voice pissed off state legislators so much that they pretty much gave him what he wanted just to get rid of him. His name was usually preceded by the phrase "that asshole," as in "that asshole Ken Thomas." Even a few respectable women were known to use it from time to time. And then giggle because being so bawdy gave them an exhilarating sense of naughtiness and freedom.

Now he stood in Matthews's door, obviously having bypassed Rafferty out front. Rafferty showed up moments later. He loomed behind the short, narrow, gaudily dressed mayor, looking apologetic. Thomas would be talking to you and just bolt to the back so that he could pop in unexpectedly on the sheriff, catching him unawares, it seemed, as if the lawman might be caught in a violent nose-picking moment, or even—God help us— defiling himself in a carnal way.

Matthews was, in point of fact, stacking up his mail preparatory to pitching most of it in his wastebasket.

"Afternoon, Reed."

"Afternoon, Mayor."

"I hope I'm not bothering you."

"I'm just sitting here upholding the Constitution and the American way. Nothing I can't do while I'm talking to you."

Mayor Ken Thomas didn't have a sense of humor. He looked confused by Matthews's joke. He also looked irritated. He obviously assumed that just about everything

Matthews said to him was some form of sarcasm. The two men had never liked each other.

Matthews said, as Rafferty disappeared, heading back to the front, "Sit down, Mayor. But please don't ask me about that endorsement. I haven't changed my mind. I'm still thinking it over."

Elections here were in late September. Even given all he'd done for the town, the mayor was facing a tough re-election. His imperious manner had finally begun to weary a majority of the people.

"You're still thinking it over? Hell, Matthews, the election's in two weeks." He seated himself as he said this.

"I know when the election is, Mayor. I just don't feel comfortable endorsing anybody." The thing was, next year when his own term was up, he'd maybe have to ask somebody like Ken Thomas here for his own endorsement.

"I heard you were thinking of endorsing my opponent."

Matthews smiled. "C'mon, now, Mayor. You didn't hear any such thing and you know it." *Your opponent is just as big an idiot as you are*, Matthews wanted to say. But couldn't, of course.

The sweaty little man leaned forward, seeming to burst from the cheap checkered type of suit common to drummers, and said, "There's a town hall meeting next Monday, Matthews. That'd be a perfect place to endorse me. And by the way, neither you nor Rafferty have offered me a cup of coffee."

"You want a cup of coffee?"

"No. But I'd appreciate being offered one."

Pure Ken Thomas. Pure waste of time.

Matthews shrugged. "You know something? And this is the truth. We've both got more than our share of enemies in this town. I don't know why you think my endorsement would be all that useful to you. In some places, it'd probably even *lose* you votes."

"In other words, you're not going to endorse me."

Matthews shrugged, deciding to get it over with. "In other words, I'm not going to endorse you. I'm not going to endorse anybody."

Ken Thomas's blue eyes shone with malicious glee. He said, "Then I won't feel bad about ordering up a night patrol."

"A what?"

"A night patrol. Two unsolved murders. Every citizen in this town hiding behind locked doors at night. Women and small children living in fear."

"You sound like a dime novel about the yellow peril."

"You don't get the complaints I do. My office is packed tight every day with people wanting to know when it'll be safe to live here again."

That meant two old biddies from First Lutheran had visited his office to complain about the killings, Matthews thought.

"So what will this night patrol do exactly?"

"Think about each word separately, Sheriff. And you'll be able to figure it out. Night — they work at night. And patrol — they patrol."

"And what do they patrol?"

"The streets. *Our* streets. The streets of the best town in the entire West."

"In other words, a cheap election ploy."

"I don't like your tone."

"I don't like your dumb ideas. You send half-a-dozen men half-liquored up into the streets at night, you're going to get trouble."

"Correction, Sheriff. The law-abiding citizens of this town don't get trouble. The gunnies and the Indian warriors and the white slavers, they're the ones who get trouble. And they get it from the night patrol."

"Gunnies? There hasn't been a gunny here since before *I* got here. And the Indians are all on reservations now, the poor bastards. And white slavers—*what* white slavers? You're reading the *Police Gazette* again. There's never been a white slaver in this town and never will be for the simple reason that the citizens here are good people and they'd shoot anybody who even *thought* about being a white slaver."

"That's just what I expected, Sheriff. Your typical head-in-the-sand attitude. We have a crime spree and you look the other way."

Matthews was getting angrier than he wanted to. His usual approach to Thomas's vote-getting schemes was to smile until they went away. Thomas mostly just liked to come in here and try and rattle Matthews. He knew Matthews didn't have any respect for him and he got at him the only way he could. By proposing ideas sure to piss off the sheriff.

"You know something, Matthews?" the mayor said,

standing up. "I don't give a damn if you endorse me or not."

Matthews smiled. "Mission accomplished."

"What's that supposed to mean?"

"It means you knew I wouldn't like your idea of a night patrol. We've got the best night patrol there is. His name is Harold Lincoln. But you knew I'd say I didn't like the idea, so now you can tell everybody that you're doing the best job you can—despite the lazy, stupid sheriff. You figure you'll get some extra votes at my expense. And maybe you will. But I'll tell you this. Any of your 'night patrol' people start firing their weapons, I'll haul them into jail. Technically, it's against the law to carry guns in town, anyway."

"Well, we'll see what people say when I tell them you won't cooperate when citizens try and make their town safe. We'll just see, Matthews."

And then, the Lord be praised, he was gone.

"Well, fancy meeting you here," Annie Reynolds said. The wicker basket she carried was filled with groceries. In her blue gingham dress and blue hair ribbon, she looked like a girl in her teens shopping for her mother. The imp was still in her chocolate brown eyes.

Matthews nodded. "Just headed over to the courthouse."

"Your life is about as exciting as mine."

"It's actually more exciting than I'd like," he said. "Two murders back-to-back isn't fun for anybody."

The dark eyes were shadowed for a moment, cloud covering sun. He wondered why. It was easy to misread expressions. Her odd, slightly troubled look might have been coincidental, but he didn't think so. "That's not much fun to think about, is it? Murder, I mean," she added.

"The mayor's going to start a night patrol."

"What a joke he is."

"They keep reelecting him."

He was just about to say more about the mayor when he realized why she'd suddenly looked troubled. Nothing to do with the subject of the two murders. Something to do with the stranger standing behind him and to the right on the sidewalk. The one who'd been at the inquest. She'd seen him and then glanced back at Matthews. Now she was looking at the stranger again. The man wasn't any more imposing than he'd been earlier, when Matthews had seen him at her door. But there was something about him that disturbed her, that was obvious.

"Well," she said. "I guess I'd better be on my way. I'm baking biscuits this afternoon."

He angled himself so that he could see the man. "Looks like you've made another conquest."

She blushed. He'd never seen her blush before. It gave her a vulnerability, a sweetness. "Oh, he's not interested in me that way."

"Then how's he interested in you?" He smiled, to take the harshness from his question. He sounded more like a lawman than a friend.

"He's just somebody I knew a long time ago. Just passing through town."

"He giving you any trouble?"

She forced a smile. "There you go. Being sheriff. Have to know everybody and everything, don't you?"

"Force of habit." He hesitated. "So who is he?"

"I don't really have to answer that."

"I know. I was just asking."

"No, you weren't. You were being a lawman, like I said. And in fact, I don't think I'll answer your damned ole question at all. It's none of your business who he is or what he means to me. Now, are you going to arrest me for that?"

She glared at him, gripped the wicker basket of groceries tighter in her small hand, and then hurried away.

SEVEN

AFTER SUPPER AT the café, Matthews went back to his office. Late in the afternoon word had traveled that tonight the "night patrol" would gather and spread throughout the town, bringing peace and justice and safety. Matthews and Harold Lincoln might be joking about it, but there seemed to be a favorable sentiment for the patrol among citizens.

"You go on home and relax," Lincoln told Matthews around eight o'clock. "I can handle things here."

"You just go on and do what you'd normally do. I'll stay in the office and if you need any backup, let me know."

"You shouldn't have to pull two shifts."

"Harold, why do you think they pay me all that money?"

"I thought you made all your money because you had to put up with that idiot mayor."

"Well, that, too, but mostly they've made me rich just because I pull double shifts every once in a while."

Lincoln laughed. "I'm glad to know that." They'd both been bitching about money lately — the town council had recently included a lot of money for statues of various kinds but no raises for anybody in the sheriff's department — and joked about the subject whenever they got the chance. "Really, though, Sheriff, you don't need to stay. They'll find out how cold it is tonight and all be home in bed before ten."

"I doubt that. The mayor was over at the Red Dog giving them a big talk when I came back from the café. And they were all pretty liquored up by then."

"Anything you could arrest them for?"

"Nothing I could think of. And I gave it some serious thought. That's why I'm going to sit right here till I know they're all back home in their beds where they belong."

When the clock chimed nine, Lincoln stood up, yawned, stretched, walked over, and poured himself half a cup of coffee. "I need to get a little agitated to stay awake tonight."

"Well, that's the stuff that'll do it. It'll agitate the hell out of you, in fact."

Harold finished his coffee in two swallows. "I wish I could arrest the mayor."

"Now there's a thought."

"Put him in that cell back there and listen to him yell all night. That'd be a lot of fun." Another yawn. "Well, I'd better head out. I'll do my rounds first and then check out the saloons. Then I'll catch up with the patrol." He smiled at Matthews. "You know, that mayor of ours really is an idiot."

"Amen to that."

The mayor wore a six-gun and a white Stetson that appeared to be half as tall as he was. The eight men in front of him, like the mayor, had all had a mite too much liquor over to the Red Dog and were all too het up to catch themselves some killers. A few of them carried torches, which played hell staying lighted in the steady winds.

The mayor, who was not without mental resources when it came to cunning, tramped his troops up the main street, all the way to the town limits to the east. This gave a majority of the voters a chance to see how he'd bravely assembled an impressive team of town-protectors and was dispersing them throughout the neighborhoods. You could see little kids in windows, watching the drunks with the torches marching up the middle of the street. The kids watched with awe. Their parents were about equally divided—respect and appreciation from one half; smirks and cynicism from the other.

Then the group dispersed. Each man had a vague memory of the places he'd been assigned tonight. And by God, he took his gun and he went there. Making the night safe for innocents and the American way once again.

The fun had just begun.

Good thing Matthews had stayed in the office, because by ten o'clock that night good, hardworking citizens began filing into the sheriff's office with their complaints.

Mrs. Cooper was mad because one of the men of the patrol had tramped all over her daffodils; Mr. Meyers threatened to sock Bob Farner from the patrol in the nose because he'd found Farner urinating in his backyard while at the same time lifting a pint of rye into his mouth; Mrs. Heckler claimed she would institute a lawsuit against Cosmo Baines because he accidentally stepped on one of her new kittens and broke its tiny leg, though she wasn't at all sure about the "accidental" part; and Mr. Ruthie Knowles (or so he was known behind his back, the sarcasm warranted because Dave Knowles was the most henpecked man in the valley) insisted that two members of the patrol were peeping in the bedroom window while Ruthie was in various stages of undress.

There were a couple of other complaints, too. Matthews wrote them down with great relish. He looked forward to presenting them to the mayor tomorrow morning.

Between complaints, he went back and spent a couple of minutes with Ab Soames. "Any luck yet?"

"I'm feeling good about it. But nothing clear yet."

It was a pretty damned frustrating business, the human mind. Here Ab knew who the killer was, but he couldn't get his memory to cooperate. It was right there and yet it wasn't right there. It was lost, maybe permanently, in Ab's brain. Maybe it would stay there forever. Or maybe it was all bullshit. Maybe Ab was the killer and he just didn't want to admit it to himself. Or maybe he had already admitted it to himself but was using this memory business as a ruse so the sheriff here might think he was innocent. None of it made sense and all of it made sense and none of it made sense.

Matthews went back up front. No more complaints, it seemed. Maybe Harold's prediction had come true. The chafing cold weather had deterred the night patrol from its appointed rounds.

He had some of the coffee Harold had disparaged. And understood instantly *why* Harold had disparaged it. Sometimes the day folks ran out of coffee and Rafferty took it upon himself to brew up some more. All the Indian wars could have been won simply if Rafferty had just served the Indians coffee. They wouldn't have died but they sure would have wished they had.

He was just choking down the last of the cup when a cannonball seemed to come ripping through the center of the door. It was Pug Malone, the winner of many strongman contests out at the county fair. He was big strong stuff despite the face that made him look like he was ten. "You better come, Sheriff. It's Harold."

"Harold?" Matthews got one of those instant terrible feelings that scared him up and down his entire body, his stomach knotting so tight his bowels groaned. "What the hell happened?"

"Somebody shot him and he ain't in very good shape."

Darkness. Rushing. Pug and Matthews running beside each other like kids in a race. Way too fast to talk. Dark thoughts filling Matthews's mind. The kind of rage and panic that consumes all else. Find the sonofabitch who shot Harold. Kick him within an inch of his life.

Then take him all the way to the other side with several
bullets in the face and chest. Human beings didn't come
any better than Harold and some fucker was going to pay
the biggest price of all.

The middle of the street. The stupid night patrol
forming a semicircle around a body in the dust. Lanterns
held high. The mayor standing nearest the body. Shrink-
ing back as he saw Matthews approach. Patting his forehead with his handkerchief. Looking desperately around
at his foolish stupid-ass so-called patrol. His expression
saying that he hoped they would defend him.

The most startling sight of all was the mortuary
wagon, Timothy G. Bevens, official town ghoul, standing off to the side. Smiling, for God's sake, as Matthews
approached the group.

No time for talk. Matthews dropped to a knee next to
Harold's body. "Give me that lantern," Matthews
snapped.

One of the night patrol leaned away—as if he expected Matthews to jump to his feet and pound him into
the ground—but handed his lantern to the lawman.

Matthews held the lantern close to the face of his
friend. Harold was unconscious, his face gleaming with
sweat. Matthews found a faint pulse in his throat. Foamy
spittle leaked from the right side of Harold's mouth. The
wound itself was to the left of the heart. The blood had
darkened Harold's tan flannel shirt. It was too cold for
flying insects. The only buzzard was the mortuary man.

"We need to get him to Doc McGinty's," Matthews
said. He stood up. Knees cracking. He shouted to
Bevens. "Get your wagon over here, Bevens."

"I'm sorry, Sheriff. But he ain't dead."

"I didn't ask for your medical opinion. I asked for your wagon. Now get it over here."

"I tote dead bodies, Sheriff. Not live ones. I'm not no ambulance."

Not even Matthews knew he could move with such fury or force. In eight blurred steps, he seized the mortuary man by the collar and began slamming the back of his head against the side of the wagon seat. There were few times in his life when Matthews had wanted to know what it was like to kill somebody. This was one of those times. It was completely irrational, completely unjustifiable, but he didn't give a shit. Here was a man who refused to help another man, a man who might be dying. A sanctimonious "Christian" who sure didn't remind Matthews at all of the real Jesus.

He forced himself to stop. He let go of Bevens's lapels and let the man slip to the ground.

"Pug, can you drive this wagon to the doc's?"

"I sure can, Sheriff."

"Thanks." He glared at a couple of the patrol members. "Two of you help Pug get Harold here into the wagon."

The two he was scowling at knew better than to challenge him in any way. They'd just seen what he'd done to Bevens.

When Harold was loaded onto the wagon, and when the wagon pulled away, Matthews went over to the mayor and said, "Which one of your idiots shot him?"

The mayor came to sputtering life. "Now you got no reason to go around calling these good citizens of ours—"

Matthews was inches from the mayor's face. He shouted into it, repeating the question.

Behind him a voice said, "My brother shot him, Sheriff. But he didn't mean to. He seen somebody else and got confused."

One of the burdens of being a lawman, or at least a good lawman, was that circumstances sometimes forced you to feel a little bit sorry for people you hated on principle. These men had been rounded up by a cynical politician as part of a reelection stunt. They had to take responsibility for their own actions, yes. But that they'd been used by the mayor—these weren't the smartest men around—forced Matthews to calm down a bit. He'd deal with the mayor later.

Matthews faced Don Prewitt, a farmer generally considered to be, like his brother, a bit "slow." He wasn't a mean man, but he got in trouble by letting others encourage him to do things they were afraid to. He was so reckless with fireworks, for instance, that he'd been banned from even showing up at Fourth of July festivities.

"Where's Con now?"

"Out in back in the gazebo."

"You men wait here."

This was the first time that Matthews had taken note that the house they were in front of was Bryce Harlow's colonial mansion. The two-story house gleamed white in the gloom. Every window in the front of the house showed light. Passing by the largest windows, he had a glimpse of Harlow standing inside in the living room. He had a rifle in his hand. He was no doubt scared, of the night patrol if nothing else.

He heard Con-for-Conrad Prewitt before he saw him. The man was crying. He sounded young. Matthews resented Con's tears. He wanted to hate the sonofabitch clean and pure. But the tears made that impossible.

Matthews went up inside the gazebo and sat on a chair facing Con, who, like his brother, was dressed in overalls and a butternut jacket. Con had his face in his hands. He didn't seem to be aware of Matthews.

Matthews rolled a smoke and when he got it going, he said, "Tell me what happened, Con."

It took a minute, but Con finally raised his heavy, tear-shiny face and stared through the gloom at the lawman. "I didn't see you there, Sheriff. Is Harold gonna be all right? I didn't mean to shoot him. I thought he was the other one."

"Who was 'the other one,' Con?" Matthews said. He kept his voice gentle, neutral. This was the appropriate way to handle somebody like Con, at least for now.

"The one I seen peekin' in the window."

"When was this?"

Con snuffled up some tears and wiped his nose on the sleeve of his jacket. "We split up."

"Who split up?"

"Everybody on the night patrol. The mayor, he had the whole town divided up, see? And we was each to take a square, the way he had it drawed on his map."

"All right. And you took this section of town?"

"Uh-huh. Me'n my brother."

"So you were checking on houses and making sure nobody suspicious was around them."

"Uh-huh. Just like the way you say, Sheriff, that's just

what we was doin'. And I got up behind Mr. Harlow's house here and I seen this here man at the window and—and I wasn't sure what to do."

"Why didn't you just yell at him, scare him away?"

"Well, I—" He hesitated. "You know what people say about me, Sheriff. That I ain't too smart upstairs. So I didn't want to do nothin' wrong. So I run to see if I could find my brother. He's sort of the brains in the family."

"I see." The brains in the family, Matthews thought. And hated the mayor all the more for using men like these. But that's the way the world ran. The powerful people used the powerless to do their fighting and dying for them, pumping them up with lies and hatred to make them feel important and superior. And then hiding in their mansions when the gunplay started. "So you went and got your brother."

"Uh-huh. And he said we should shoot him. Not kill him. Just shoot him. And take him in."

"But when you got back there, you saw who you thought was the intruder but it turned out to be Harold."

He lowered his head again. "Mr. Harlow come out and told us—after I shot Harold—that he'd had Harold come out here to check on a prowler. That's why Harold was around back of the house. And that's why I shot him." He raised his head. "What're you gonna do to me, Sheriff?"

Matthews stood up. "I'm going to trust you for tonight, Con."

"Trust me?"

"I'm going to let you go home and see your wife and

kids and sleep at home tonight. Then I want you to be at my office at eight o'clock tomorrow morning."

"You gonna put me in jail?"

"I'm not sure yet."

"I honest didn't mean to shoot him."

"That's the worst thing of all," Matthews said. "I know you didn't mean to shoot him. But you shouldn't have been out here with a gun prowling around in the first place."

"But it was the mayor's idea, Sheriff."

"Yeah," Matthews said, almost savoring the bitterness in his tone. "It was the mayor's idea."

By now, the mayor had vanished, most likely to spend a long night conniving an explanation for the townspeople, finding somebody to blame the folly of his night patrol on. This just might be the most difficult lie the mayor had ever been forced to contrive. If Harold hadn't been shot, this would be funny, the mayor so desperate and all.

Matthews grabbed a lantern and went around to the back of the mansion. He spent ten minutes on his haunches examining the ground around the window where Harold had been shot. The ground was still damp from the recent rains. While footprints were lost in the grass, they showed up clearly in a foot-wide fringe of mud at the edge of the house itself. He went over and over these carefully, making sure that his first impression had been accurate.

There were two sets of prints here, definitely. Harold's big feet were unmistakable. Size thirteen wide. The other prints were probably around size eight or nine.

Both sets of prints were about equally fresh and equally clear.

He spent a little time reconstructing what might have happened. Harold sees somebody at Bryce Harlow's window and tries to sneak up on him. Just about the time Harold is ready to reach the man, Con, drunk, his eyes confused by the darkness, decides to help Harold out. He fires. Except he doesn't hit the intruder. He hits Harold.

Maybe that wasn't exactly the way it happened, Matthews thought. But it was likely something on that order. Con wasn't a mean man, but he was certainly reckless after a few beers. And so, with all the best intentions in the world, he starts firing away.

Matthews went to the back door and knocked.

"What a mess," Bryce Harlow said when he opened the door for Matthews. "What a terrible, horrible mess." He wore a silk robe and carried a Peacemaker.

"Right now, Harlow, all I care about is my deputy. I want to know what's going on with you and your friends. Judging by the footprints near one of your windows over there, Harold saw somebody and went to investigate. Apparently Con Prewitt saw him, too. That's why he opened fire and hit Harold by mistake. Now I want you to tell me what's going on here. Who's after you?"

"After me?" Harlow smiled. "Sheriff, nobody's 'after me.' I'm a businessman. There're some people who don't like me, sure. Everybody's disliked by somebody. But nobody's 'after me.' What we're talking about is some prowler. I'm a successful man. A prowler—or a thief, I guess you'd call him—he could find a lot of things to steal in here. That's what he was doing here, I'm sure."

"Nobody's going to break in while you're home. With all the lights on and you sitting in the living room."

"Well, then, I guess we have a mystery on our hands, don't we? I have no idea why anybody'd be peeking in my windows. He sure wouldn't get much of a show. The Harlow family is a very modest family. I'm afraid he'd be terribly disappointed."

He was a smooth liar. He'd seemed a bit shaken when he first came to the door, but once he began evading Matthews's questions, he managed to sound almost truthful.

"Gerry Soames dies. A Pinkerton man dies. And now you've got a prowler."

"And you're saying what, Sheriff? That these three are connected? I'm afraid I'd have to disagree. Ab Soames is an unstable drunkard and I don't know anybody except you who was surprised that he killed poor Gerry. He's a shiftless, resentful bastard who deserves whatever justice he gets. The Pinkerton man I don't know anything about. But I do know this—nobody's 'after me.' This is all a coincidence tonight."

Matthews shrugged. "I guess the only thing that's going to change your mind is if this prowler of yours manages to shoot you. If you live through it, then you'll tell me all about it. I just hope it won't be too late, Harlow."

"I appreciate your concern, Matthews. I really do."

But he was already closing the door, leaving the lawman alone in the darkness.

•   •   •

It came every night. Every single night. It didn't matter if he was drunk or sober, in a good mood or a bad one, sleepy or ready to go out and have some fun. There was probably a word for it — some kind of medical word — but if there was, Paul Reynolds didn't know it. He just knew the effects of it.

He sat on the edge of his bed in the cheap hotel, listening to people cough, sneeze, snore, laugh, curse, sex a woman, masturbate. The latter was so lonely, he didn't like to think about it. All his life preachers and doctors had warned him about masturbation. How it took its toll on everything from eyesight to sanity. But what they didn't warn you about was the loneliness that accompanied the shame afterward. A kind of loneliness that fed into the night moods he dreaded — that feeling of being utterly alone, of having failed at every aspect of living, of wanting the courage just to end it all. It was beyond tears, the entire experience. Tears would be a relief, a momentary escape. But he never cried, no matter how bad the mood got, he never cried. It was as if he didn't know how.

He had hoped that these night moods would dissipate when he went after Gerald Soames and his friends. But even that had not worked out as he'd planned. Something strange was going on in this town and he needed to find out what.

He lay in the darkness now, listening to the people on either side of him. Thin walls. You could hear it all. He imagined that each tiny room was like a cage in a zoo. This entire hotel floor a zoo of the lonely and dispossessed.

He thought of his sister Annie accusing him of the murders. If she only knew; if she only knew.

Hector Nolan said, there in his own darkness, "I'm getting shingles again."

"Honey, you always think you're getting shingles again," his wife Azalea said. She was a stout woman who had long ago gotten used to her husband's rather delicate nature. You couldn't even mention a malady without Hector claiming he had it five minutes later. She hid all magazines and newspapers from him that contained any medical references at all. But of all maladies possible, his obsession was with shingles. He'd actually had a minor case of them once, a scaly patch, much like a bad scrape at the scabbing stage, on his back. Maybe the size of a playing card. It had been painful, it had been ugly, it had been, for him, intolerable and proof positive that his body had turned into a mortal enemy.

The entire event had taken eight days. No diva had ever performed a grand opera more grand than Hector had during those days. He took to bed; he had her daub on the ointment the doc had given him far more frequently than the doc recommended; and he had forced her to examine every inch of his body—including certain hidden and hairy parts she would rather have been spared—twice a day to see if the shingles were making an appearance elsewhere on his scarecrowlike body.

Nerves, the doctor had said, that was the cause of shingles. My Lord, she wished he hadn't said that. Now every time Hector got upset about something, he immediately felt an assault of shingles coming on.

"Just go to sleep, dear."

"He had a prowler tonight."

"Who had a prowler tonight, dear?"

"Bryce."

"And how would you know that? You haven't been out tonight."

"The door. You were getting ready for bed. One of Bryce's workers had been out to the house tonight and came by here to let me know. Bryce had a prowler and Harold Lincoln got shot."

"Oh, poor Harold. He's such a nice man. Is he all right? You said shot, you didn't say killed. When people say 'shot' and not 'killed', I always assume the person's going to be all right."

"He isn't dead, anyway."

"Did they catch the prowler who shot him?"

"The prowler didn't shoot him. Con Prewitt shot him."

"Con Prewitt? Oh, he's a terrible man. He and his brother. I'm not surprised he turned out to be a prowler."

"He wasn't the prowler. He was part of the night patrol."

"He wasn't the prowler and he shot poor Harold, anyway? Well, I must say, I'm not surprised, dear. I'm not surprised by *any*thing those Prewitts would do. And what's the night patrol?"

But he was finished with talking, explaining. Explaining things to Azalea was endless. She had to know every detail.

"I'll tell you in the morning," he said.

"No good-night kiss, dear?"

He sighed.

"And I wish you'd tell me what's been troubling you so much lately, dear. Maybe it's something I could help you with."

He sighed the sigh of an old and ancient man, though he wouldn't be even sixty for three years yet.

Rolling over to face her seemed like such a difficult task suddenly. He was drained completely. All he could think of was: *My turn will come. He'll come after me just the way he came after old Gerry. Just the way he came after Bryce tonight. He'll come back for Bryce again. He won't let one little failure stop him. It'll probably just make him mad. Make him want to kill us all the more.*

He rolled over, of course—hell to pay if he didn't—and kissed her, remembering long, long ago when she wouldn't have needed to ask for a good-night kiss. Long, long ago when he would have been all over her for no good reason at all. What a beauty she'd been.

Long, long ago.

EIGHT

SOMEBODY WAS BULLSHITTING him and he didn't like it.

That was the thought uppermost in Matthews's mind as he tried unsuccessfully to get to sleep that night. Maybe—and only maybe—the dead Pinkerton didn't have anything to do with the murder of Gerald Soames or whatever the hell was going on with Bryce Harlow. But somebody was withholding vital information and when he woke up in the morning—assuming that he ever got to sleep—he planned to visit Harlow and get some truthful answers.

His only satisfaction as he lay there rolling, sighing, scratching, making cigarette after cigarette, was that the mayor had made a very public ass out of himself tonight. This would certainly work against him in the upcoming election. There'd been a time in the West—before a true unified and systematic system of justice had been put into place — when vigilantism had been accepted at least passively. But as the new century neared, vigilantism of any form was getting to be unpopular. A couple of innocent men had been lynched not too long ago up in the northern part of the state, and people still remembered that. The "night patrol" would seem just as foolish and reckless to the townspeople here. Matthews was sure of that.

He finally slept sometime around four o'clock. He'd been thinking about Karen Davies. She was as proud and wily and unpredictable as her father. Which was funny because when she talked about herself, she always spoke as if she was this wispy, confused, uncertain young girl who was completely overwhelmed by the mean and cynical world. Which she wasn't at all. On the contrary. She also wouldn't admit that she was afraid of falling in love again. She'd been humiliated the first time and dreaded it happening to her again. Even mild Reed Matthews scared her. He considered himself pretty easy to know and trust. But maybe he was just as blind to his own nature as Karen was to hers. All he knew was that over the course of a friendship he had easily come to love her. Loved her more than he had ever loved anyone else.

Bryce Harlow said, "He was outside my back door last night. Peeking in the window. If that stupid night patrol hadn't come along, he probably would've shot me right through the window."

"You sure it was him, Bryce?" Vernon Davies asked.

"Who else would it have been, Vernon? That was a pretty stupid remark."

"This is no way to talk to each other," Hector Nolan said.

Their lives were in jeopardy. The time was 6:25 A.M. They drank coffee but hadn't yet fed their bellies. They were scared, angry, baffled still by how their sensible, comfortable lives had been turned around so quickly.

They sat in Bryce Harlow's empty suite of offices. He'd gone to each of their homes around 5:30 and summoned them to a meeting.

"I've been thinking," Davies said, pawing at his freshly shaven face. Each man had nicks and cuts on his cheeks. Shaving too quickly was a dangerous business. The clothes hadn't been put on quite right, either, a crooked collar here, a missed button there. "I know a man in Denver you can hire to take care of people like this blackmailer."

"A killer?" Nolan said.

"A former U.S. marshal who knows what he's doing," Davies said, "not some lunatic who takes lives for pleasure."

"My God, Vernon, think of what you're proposing," Bryce Harlow said.

"Don't give me one of your lectures on morality, Bryce. It's too fucking early in the morning."

"Vernon—think about it. That's all I'm saying. We're worried we'll have to go to prison if any of this comes out. But what happens if we hire a man to kill somebody? He kills him—and then that comes out, too. That's a hanging offense, Vernon, in case you've forgotten."

"Maybe hanging would be better than rotting in a cell somewhere," Vernon said.

"That's bravado," Nolan said. "At least as far as I'm concerned. I'm not ready to die yet." He hesitated. "Bryce and I had a little time to talk before you got here just now, Vernon." He looked at Harlow, then back at Vernon Davies. "We think we should pay him what he wants."

"Now that's real smart," Davies said. "We pay him once and then he starts coming back every time he needs more." He shook his head. He stood up. He was so heavy that merely rising to his feet caused him to gasp for breath. "You two can do what you want. But I won't give that bastard anything. Not one damned dollar."

He walked around the small conference table and over to the door. He looked back at them as if he wanted to say something, but then just shook his head and went out.

"Well, that went just about the way you said it would, Bryce."

"He's the most stubborn man I know. It's his pride. He doesn't care about the money. It's just the idea of giving in to somebody who holds some kind of power over him."

"You weren't very happy about paying any money the other night," Nolan reminded him.

"That was before he came to my house last night."

"Speaking of that," Nolan said, "I wonder how Harold's doing. The poor fella."

"Last I heard, Doc got the bullet out and things looked pretty good."

"You want some more coffee?"

"Thanks."

Bryce Harlow had just stood up, grabbing Nolan's cup and his own, when the three shots sounded. This early in the morning, before any heavy wagon traffic, with only the competition of roosters and a few dogs for sounds, the gunfire was not only ominous but vulgar. It had turned an elegant sunny morning filthy.

The gunshots changed Matthews's plans.

He'd been walking to his office when the shots crackled through the early morning mist that the sun had just now started to burn off. He was fired by an almost evangelical determination to get Nolan, Harlow, and Davies together in one office and demand to know what they knew. He felt good about this. They couldn't resist him much longer. He was, for all of his many shortcomings, for all his poverty and lack of formal education, the law in this town.

But the gunshots — stunning, coarse, paralyzing — changed his plans instantly.

Annie Reynolds was just finishing her breakfast of biscuits and coffee when she heard — as did the rest of the just-risen town — the three quickly consecutive shots that destroyed the early morning peace.

It was funny. You'd think that living in the West this way, you'd get used to gunfire. There was so much of it at times. The booming sound of it seemed to be everywhere. But the opposite was true, at least with Annie. It was a code for things gone suddenly amiss. Maybe if she lived outside of town where hunting and target practice were common. But not in town like this.

Two possible explanations for the gunfire came to her. She didn't want to contemplate either one of them for long.

Her brother Paul had been found out and the law had hunted him down and killed him.

Her brother Paul had taken aim at his next victim. A perfect time of day to do it, too. City limits. Misty morning. Few people up and about yet. Escape easy.

She didn't know which possible explanation was worse.

She loved her brother. Disturbed as he was, after what he'd done the law would have no choice but to kill him. Maybe cutting him down this way was better than making him—and her—go through a humiliating public trial and ending up on the gallows for everybody to see.

But as much as she loved her brother, she didn't want him to kill again. And if he'd done that this morning . . .

She wanted to stay in her small cottage. She didn't ever want to leave. She didn't want to find out which it had been—Paul being killed, or Paul killing somebody.

But there was no choice. Either way, she had to find Reed Matthews now and tell him the truth.

The first person Matthews saw on the sidewalk out in front of Bryce Harlow's office building was Vernon Davies's accountant, Roy Fuller. The man sat on the edge of the boardwalk, his head pressed against his hand, his elbow balanced on his knee. He appeared to be in a mild state of shock. He kept muttering to himself and shaking his head. He'd had a bad couple of days.

The other night he'd been robbed and now, obviously, something even worse had taken place.

"What happened, Roy?" Matthews said.

Behind him, from every direction, Matthews could hear the sound of footsteps padding across the dusty street. The town was alive now, throwing on clothes, running out to see what had happened — wanting to know and not wanting to know. What if it had been somebody they'd known and liked?

Fuller raised his head. He managed to look very young and very old at the same time. "He's dead."

"Who's dead?"

"Vernon. Vernon Davies."

"Sonofabitch." But Matthews wasn't thinking of Vernon Davies. He was thinking of Karen Davies. And what her eyes would look like when she learned of her father's death.

"Out back," Fuller said. He was all suited up for the day. He'd even splashed on bay rum and oiled his hair down flat. All ready for a day at the office, and then this. "Out back, he was taking the alley by our office. He did that sometimes when he dropped in on Bryce Harlow. Somebody was waiting for him there."

"Sonofabitch," Matthews said again, sounding as shocked as Fuller, "sonofabitch."

Then he strode back to the alley to find out exactly what had happened.

Karen Davies was helping the maid open two large Sears and Roebucks boxes that had arrived late yesterday. The maid had needed some new everyday dishes. There were plenty of special-occasion dishes, but the ordinary ones had gradually been broken and had dwindled down to four in number. The maid, Carmella, suffered increasingly from arthritic pain in her fingers, the shape of which was gnarled and ugly. Some days she had a difficult time grasping so much as an empty cup, which explained how so many of the ordinary plates had gotten broken. The logical thing would be to let her go — which Vernon Davies had suggested to Karen several times — but Carmella had a heart condition and couldn't work at her former speed. So Karen found the time most days to help the woman around the house. Carmella was so appreciative of this that she would sometimes, without any apparent reason, seize Karen's delicate hand in her cramped own and say "Thank you" while tears filled her eyes.

The dishes had come packed in a heavy crate. Karen used the claws of a hammer to pull back the wooden slats.

She had just started lifting the boxed and paper-cushioned plates from inside the crate when the shots came. Three of them.

Later on in the day, Karen would think back and recall that at the very instant she'd heard the shots, she knew that her father was dead. There was no rational explanation for this. But when she'd dressed and walked down the hall this morning, she found his door open and the bedroom empty. He wasn't downstairs, either. She also realized, hearing the shots and knowing that her father was dead, that the gunfire had to do with the mysterious letter they'd been arguing about, the letter that had sunk him into anxiety and gloom.

Her first reaction, after setting the hammer down on the edge of the crate, was to put a slender hand to her breast and feel her mind start to go fuzzy and faint.

Carmella, seeing this, grabbed the slender girl and held her tight to her. She was glad she could be a help to Karen, even if she had no idea what had upset the girl so suddenly.

NINE

VERNON DAVIES WAS dead.

The killer hadn't taken any chances. He'd taken off the back of Davies's head at fairly close range with two shots and then put a bullet into his back, just below the left shoulder blade. Davies lay facedown in the narrow, dirt-floored alley, his massive hand with its massive ruby pinkie ring splayed across a relatively fresh pile of horse manure. The sight of this was unseemly enough to Matthews that he toed the hand away from the greenish splash of feces.

The usual crew was on hand, and sooner than usual because the killing had been right in the middle of town itself. The mortuary man, the doc, the newspaperman. And the crowd. What a way to start a workday, Matthews thought. Who could concentrate on work after seeing Vernon Davies dead in an alley like this?

When Doc McGinty got done looking him over, he came over to Matthews and said, "Well, at least he wasn't in any pain. Not for more than a second, anyway. You going to tell Karen yourself?"

"Guess I'll have to." He paused, starting to make plans for talking to any possible eyewitnesses. "How's Harold?"

"He had a pretty good night, all things considered." McGinty squinted up at Matthews. "What the hell's going on in this town all of a sudden?"

But before Matthews could answer, his deputy Rafferty tapped him on the shoulder. "Davies here was coming from a meeting at Bryce Harlow's office."

"Pretty early for a meeting. I take it you talked to him and Nolan?"

"Yeah. They don't look too good. They took it pretty hard."

No wonder, Matthews thought. Though he still didn't know what was going on, he knew by now that somebody was shooting and killing members of the group that basically ran this town. "They still at Harlow's?"

"No. They left when I did. Said they were going home, both Harlow and Nolan."

"Thanks," Matthews said. "Start asking if anybody might have seen the shooting. Or at least seen somebody besides Davies in the alley."

"Somebody sure hates these fellas," Rafferty said.

"They sure do," Matthews said. "You handle things here for now, Rafferty. I need to go see Karen Davies in a few minutes."

"How'd you like to hear that your father's been killed? That's a hell of a note this early in the morning." Rafferty turned back to the crowd, started walking among them, asking his lawman questions.

Three men loaded the body of Vernon Davies onto the wagon. As Matthews watched this, Doc said, "Rafferty was right. Somebody's sure got it in for Davies and his cohorts. Wonder what it's all about."

"Well, one way or the other, this morning I'm going to find out what it's all about." Matthews heard early morning crankiness in his voice. He needed to steady himself before he went to see Karen Davies. Right now all he wanted to do was get Harlow and Nolan in a room somewhere and slap them around until they told him the truth.

The back doors of various businesses started opening, merchants peeking out to see what was going on. Broom in hand, pencil behind the ear, smudgy apron tied around the waist—the merchants prepared themselves for a slow morning if not a slow day. The killing would likely bring a lot of people to town to gawk around and listen to all the bullshit theories that came tumbling out between batwing doors—but that kind of crowd never spent much except on beer and tobacco. The respectable people would just go on about their day. But there weren't enough respectable people in town to make a merchant's day. For that, you needed a whole lot of unrespectable people, too.

On his way to the Davies place, he saw Annie Reynolds rushing toward him. He could see that she hadn't spent much time getting herself ready to go outside. Her hair was mussed and her shirt and jeans soiled. If she was aware of these things, she obviously didn't care.

"I need to talk to you, Reed. I should've talked to you before they started getting killed." Up close, he could see how exhaustion lined her face, smudged the flesh beneath her eyes.

"You know something about this?"

"Everything about this, Reed," she said, sounding as if she was about to start crying. "Everything."

He had to weigh his duties. He wanted to tell Karen personally. It was important to him. Maybe it was just a ploy to ingratiate himself with her. He wasn't sure. And he didn't give a damn. He wanted the news of her father to come from his lips.

On the other hand, it was clear that Annie wasn't just being dramatic. Annie was a practical, sensible young woman. If she said she knew "everything," then she damned well did.

"I need to talk to Karen," he said.

"She doesn't know yet?"

"I don't think so."

"That poor woman. She's always been so nice to regular folks like me."

"Why don't you walk along with me? You can tell me as we walk."

"God, Reed, I should've told you sooner."

"Well, how about telling me now?"

"It's my brother."

"Your brother? I didn't even know you had a brother."

He started walking and she fell into step next to him.

"Oh," she said, "I have a brother all right. He's the one who's been killing everybody."

PART THREE

ONE

THERE HAD ALWAYS been trouble with banks. Sometimes, the owners were crooked; other times, they were robbed so often they were useless as a repository of uninsured money; and sometimes, they simply incurred debt to the extent that they couldn't keep their doors open. Hector Nolan was a businessman—he was a businessman of some renown in this part of the country—a generally honest man who paid generally honest prices and treated all his help with a decency that was remarkable.

Hector Nolan kept a good deal of his cash in a safe at home. He had worked too hard to trust much of it to the precarious practices of a bank. In the attic, inside a safe that had taken four men to wrestle up the stairs, inside a closet that was cobwebbed and dusty because Nolan wouldn't let his wife, let alone the maid, set foot in it . . .

there resided, like a squat black steel god, a safe he'd had shipped all the way from New York City itself. The armies of Genghis Khan, Sitting Bull, and Ulysses S. Grant combined could not open this safe. He was fond of it in an almost sexual way, patting, rubbing, stroking it for long minutes at a time. Yessir, by God, let's see some gunslick sonofabitch break into *this* safe. They'd drive themselves crazy. And they'd still be trying when the sheriff and his deputies surrounded them with shotguns and led them away.

He never simply squatted down on his haunches to work the combination. He knelt down on both knees, as if praying before a god.

The safe came open within moments. He eased back the door and there before him was a wide shadowy interior packed to overflowing with paper money. It was banded in one-thousand- and five- and ten-thousand-dollar packets. He took ten of the ten-thousand-dollar packets and fitted them as flat as possible inside the pockets of his suit coat.

And then he sneezed so violently, he hurt his neck. That was the only bad thing about this attic shrine he'd built to his money. The dust. It always assaulted his allergies and sinuses, so much so that he went through the rest of the day red-eyed and raspy-voiced.

Today was going to be no exception. He knelt there with his handkerchief out and proceeded to turn the white linen a faint green color. Someday he'd have to do some dusting up here himself. He'd planned—he'd pledged—to do some dusting up here many times. But somehow it had never come to pass. He didn't like to admit it, but there was something about doing household chores that unmanned him. He'd never felt quite as manly as his friends — his damned wrists were so woman-thin and every once in a while, he realized how high-pitched his voice was — and dusting wasn't anything that was going to make him feel any more decisive or manly, that was for sure.

Just before they'd left Bryce's office, Harlow had said that he planned to stay locked inside his large colonial house, shotgun at the ready, and doing some hard, hard thinking about handling this situation. He'd said he was inclined to go to the sheriff and take his chances with the prison. Nolan had still been in shock over Vernon's death so he'd said nothing, hadn't argued at all. But now that he'd had time for some coffee — thank God his wife had gone to the farmers' market for most of the morning and he could be alone — he decided that what he'd do was take the hundred thousand to Harlow's. And tell Harlow that he was willing to pay the whole thing — every cent of it from Nolan. How could Harlow turn that down? Not a cent of it out of his own pocket. Nolan would even agree to be the one who carried the money to the place the killer would no doubt designate.

All Harlow had to do was give up on the idea of going to the sheriff. Even if they didn't go to prison, they would be shamed and shunned by the town. And that would become a prison just as binding and ugly as any concrete cell.

He went downstairs and out the door. Angled white and gleaming in the sunlit mailbox was a business envelope. Nolan plucked it free, opened it quickly, read it. The blackmailer had changed plans. Now he knew when and where he would dispose of the money. He wanted to live. To see his grandchildren. To go to his clubs. To play pinochle. Right now money didn't matter at all.

He got it and then he lost it and then he got it again and then he lost it again and wasn't that a hell of a thing, to get it and lose it so many times?

Ab Soames sat in his cell and gnawed on his fingernails. This was a major gnaw. Not a little nibbling thing that left the nails just a bit ragged. This was the kind of major gnaw that left the nails so ripped, so torn, so bloody that they'd hurt for days. Real pain. Not just a minor irritant that only stung every once in a while. This was real pain that made using his fingers difficult. He started blowing on them. Sometimes that helped. This was not an unknown ritual to him. Whenever he got this frustrated, he chawed on his nails. If you could say one thing good for drinking, that was it. You never bit your nails when you were drunk. No, sir. Drinking just took all your misery, all your dread, all your fears right away. Of course, there was always the next morning to face. . . .

He'd been at the head of the corridor again. The hallway, if you wanted to call it that. He'd been at the head of that spooky hallway again. The one in his mind. The one only he could see. The one that held the truth about the real killer. Except this time it didn't seem so long, that hallway. Except this time there seemed to be a little light on the face of the man at the other end of the hallway. Except this time there was something *really* familiar.

He knew who the real murderer was. Not by name. Not yet. But he knew he was getting closer. He knew that any time now, he'd be able to call the sheriff in and tell him the man's name. And then he'd walk out of here. Free and clear. He was sure of it.

She wasn't crying. She wasn't knitting her fingers the way she did sometimes when she got overwrought. She wasn't working her jaw the way she often did, either.

"I'll have to make all the arrangements. But Lord, I hate dealing with that damned Bevens. There's just something—unwholesome—about him."

Karen Davies wore a white blouse, black pants, low tan riding boots. Her hair was pulled back and fastened with a black ribbon.

"You can let go, you know."

They were in the sitting room. There was immense sunlight through the gauzy white curtains. They sat in facing armchairs. On the left arm of her chair sat Lazy, her gray tomcat. He was sleeping. Cats had their own dramas. Human dramas couldn't possibly be as interesting to them as their own.

"If I let go, Reed, I'll be pretty damned messy about it and you'll never get out of here. And I want you to catch him. This—Paul, was it?"

"Yes, Paul."

She shook her head. "They raped her—my father and the others—and then she stumbled and fell and hit her head."

"And died."

"And a witness saw it all."

"Yes, she was afraid to say anything. She knew that your father and Harlow and Nolan and Soames were powerful men. She's Mexican. She was afraid of them."

She eyed him almost coldly. "Do you believe all this, Reed? About my father and the others?"

"What matters is that *he* believes it, Paul Reynolds. That's why he's killing them."

"And blackmailing them."

"Yes," he said. "And blackmailing them."

"But you didn't answer my question. Do you believe it?"

"I don't know."

"They were old men."

"Not ten years ago. They would've still been in their late forties. They were on vacation, drinking."

"So you believe this story, then?"

"I don't know if I believe it or not. I'm just saying it's possible is all."

"Annie should've told you all this as soon as Soames was killed. My father would be alive if she had."

"She's aware of that. I may even press charges." He stood up. "I have to organize a manhunt."

She nodded. Looked down at Lazy. Stroked him. "You ever wish you were an animal?"

"Sometimes, I suppose. But they've got pretty rough lives."

"Not Lazy." Her voice was thick and melancholy as a sad mountain song. "He's got an easy life."

He said what she'd told him never to say. "I don't suppose I should say this now, Karen. But I love you."

She still didn't look up. She just kept right on stroking lucky Lazy. And then she said, faint as a soft breeze, "I don't suppose I should say this now, either, Reed." And then she looked up at him. "But I love you, too."

TWO

H IS NAME WAS Dick Breen. His regular job was that of timber cutter. He hired out on a daily basis freelance and did damn well for himself. He lived with a Comanche woman who was almost as antisocial as he was, which was no easy feat. His occasional other job was to draw pencil portraits of people. Give him a brush and paints and a canvas and he'd just stare at you. But put a pencil in that mightily calloused hand and he could give you a pretty close depiction of the person you described to him.

While Rafferty was assembling a posse, Matthews watched Breen draw a picture as Annie Reynolds described her brother to him. This was the stranger who'd been in town for a week or so. A lot of people had seen him including, fortunately enough, many members of the posse.

Matthews had one rule as far as pulling together a posse went. Try and get the men who begged off, or at least as many of them as possible. *Hell, I'm in the middle of plowin'; I got an appointment with the doc this morning; I hate to leave the wife alone here, her bein' pregnant and all.* Over the years, Matthews had learned that enthusiasm was a dangerous trait in a posse member. It meant he'd joined up so he could raise a little hell. This was usually the result of whiskey. A posse man or two would shove a pint in a saddlebag and be blind stiff three hours later, ready to shoot anything he imagined to be the man he was looking for. If he was drunk enough, this might mean he shot a cow, an outhouse, or even an innocent man standing in his own backyard, as had happened up to Delmar not too long ago. You usually got a wild bastard or two, but you tried to minimize their number as much as possible.

Sixteen men sat saddle when Matthews came out of the office door and started the pencil sketch moving from man to man. Annie stood in the overhang and watched it all. She was dry-eyed but forlorn. He might be a killer but he was her brother.

Rafferty had brought Matthews's horse around front. Matthews climbed up into the saddle and started pairing the men off and telling them which area they were to search. A couple of them looked disappointed. Apparently, they had their own preferred areas to look for Paul Reynolds.

Then he said, "Being part of a posse doesn't give you any special privileges. You're pretty much bound by the same laws you are as a private citizen. I don't want any

drinking and I don't want any wild shooting. You draw
that gun, you make damned sure who you're shooting at.
And just because he's on the run doesn't mean he wants
a shoot-out. A lot of men hand themselves over peaceful.
By law, you're obliged to give him that chance. You
shoot a man in cold blood—even if he's wanted for
murder—you can be charged yourself. You'd best keep
that in mind."

Sour faces showed on a few of the men. Matthews
was one of those unexciting types of lawmen. Damned
near a preacher when it came to abiding by the law.
There was a time when a posse meant having yourself a
little drunken but harmless fun. Yes, that Parsons girl
had gone and gotten herself raped by a couple posse
members back when the town was silver-crazed; and
yes, there had been that incident when a couple of other
posse members had set some teepees along the river on
fire. But it wasn't like anybody died. The Parsons gal
went on to birth six kids, and the former sheriff made
the posse members pay the Indians for setting the fire.
But hell, boys will be boys, right? Nothin' real bad had
happened.

Annie Reynolds had customers. Regular customers.
Come to pick up their candles. It seemed so absurd, so
downright ridiculous. Here all this was going on in
town—here she'd just confessed to the sheriff that her
very own brother was the killer he was looking for—and
these customers of hers kept right on coming. Knocking
on the door. Wondering if their piddling little stupid orders were ready.

As if there was nothing else more important than their piddling little stupid candles. As if a town patriarch hadn't just been gunned down; as if her very own brother wouldn't himself be gunned down very soon.

They even had smiles, the customers. Smiles and chatter. A couple of the younger men even flirted with her. They hadn't heard, obviously, and so they went on obscenely with their own obscene, absurd little lives. Eyeing her breasts; admiring her hips; brushing up against her if they got half a chance — things that would ordinarily have amused her but that now struck her as profane and infinitely silly.

And then at last the door stood silent of knocks and the doorway mute of idiotic conversation. And eyes no longer coveted her body.

She was left to go insane in her own special way.

Annie Reynolds stood up, sat down, walked around, sat down again, got up again. Once she started to cry, but then checked herself by starting to laugh. The laugh didn't last any longer than the cry. Her little brother. Her crazy little brother Paul. The men with guns were going to kill him. He probably deserved to die — no; he *did* deserve to die because he'd done some very bad things — but her blood and her heart did not understand this. Or accept it.

Her blood was his blood; her heart his heart. Scruffy little boy nobody liked; always scorned, always beaten up. There was and had always been something *wrong* with him. A glance told you that. Just the way he'd hidden their little sister from the world. As if merely by seeing what went on in the world she would be forever

soiled. Hiding her away for "protection" and not telling
Annie for days at a time where she was.

But eventually Annie learned the kind of hiding
places he preferred. High places; eyries, really; places a
princess from storybooks would hide, looking down im-
periously on her coarse and envious subjects. But they
could not see her. Oh, no, because even so much as a
glance from their filthy eyes would soil her.

High places.

He was probably in some high place now, hiding. She
started thinking of high places in and around town. She
was glad to have something to do besides nervously sit
down and jerk right back up again and then start her
crazed pacing. It had come to a fine pass in her young,
melancholy life when a laugh interrupted her tears. A lunatic for a brother; a whore for a sister. No wonder she
was so crazed.

But no, that was no good, either. Judging her brother
and sister that way. Look at how they'd been raised. For
some reason known only to God, Annie had been just a
bit stronger than her brother and sister. Just enough
stronger to deal with life as it was and not escape into the
brooding fantasies of Paul or the perfumed rooms of
whorehouses that had claimed her sister.

No reason for this other than sheer good luck. She
had nothing to gloat about, nothing to feel superior
about. She felt guilty for even once thinking that she was
better than her brother and sister.

Poor Paul. She couldn't imagine how scared he was
now, knowing that his death was drawing ever nearer.
The posse would find him. It might take a day, it might

take two. They would figure out eventually that he was in town here, hiding. And then they would keep him treed like an animal frightened of a predator and they would tell him to come down with his hands up but he would be too scared and embarrassed to do that—his shyness would come out, his paralyzing shyness—and then they would open fire and in moments he would be dead.

She had to find him, save him. Spend at least a bit of time with him before—or so she hoped—he went with her peacefully to the sheriff's office and turned himself in.

She spent the next hour trying to work, trying to give her hands something to do as she thought of all the possible hiding places Paul could find in town. There weren't many and the ones she could think of—the communal silo, the trestle bridge, the remnants of the frontier Army fort with its guard towers—none of them offered him the kind of shelter he'd need for any sustained hiding. He'd be found too quickly.

She kept on working, interrupted occasionally by a talky customer who apparently just assumed—my God, by now the story of her brother had to be all over town—that Annie would be open for business even if her cottage was on fire.

THREE

BY FOUR THAT afternoon, Paul Reynolds had been sighted eleven times in eleven different places in and around town. While the posse roamed wide across the countryside, all Matthews had time for was responding to all the hysterical sightings that were being relayed to him.

By hysterical sighting number eight, his usual polite nature was somewhat frayed, and by the time he finished off number eleven, he was damned near surly. He had traveled to all these various sites on, respectively, foot, horse, wagon. For the first two he'd gotten his hopes up. For the rest he felt nothing but barely concealed contempt.

As soon as he got back to town, Matthews went to the respective offices of Bryce Harlow and Hector Nolan. No luck. Same at their homes. He sensed they were avoiding him. They knew he was going to insist on a full explanation of what was going on.

Near sundown, he sat in his office talking to the pairs of posse members as they came back to town tired, cranky, and hungry. They'd proved to be a much better lot than he'd feared. Not a wild card among them. Not a one of them had so much as glimpsed anybody remotely resembling Reynolds, which was a hell of a lot better than all these false reports. And not a one of them had shot up an outbuilding, a farm animal, or a human being. His weariness lifted when he saw how professionally they'd behaved. This job had subtle ways of making a man cynical, and you had to guard against it lest you become one of those cold, mean bastards whose only pleasure in wearing a star was inflicting your authority on people. Nice to know you could mount a posse of decent, well-meaning citizens. Even the ones he'd worried about had come through for him.

His thoughts of capturing Reynolds alternated with his thoughts of Karen Davies. She'd never told him she loved him before this morning. Every time his mind filled with the exact timbre and richness of her voice saying those exact words, he got as giddy as a ten-year-old over a pigtailed schoolgirl who had bestowed a kiss on him. Wasn't that remarkable—a grown man, a soul-calloused man in many ways, so damned silly over love? You'd think you'd outgrow it but you never did. He'd seen seventy-year-old men arguing over the same lady. For all the death he was steeped in, for all the problems he might have catching Reynolds—he felt ridiculously wonderful. She loved him. She said so and God knows she wasn't the sort to say such a thing lightly. She loved him. But he knew her fears of marriage and wondered what her love meant exactly. Did it mean she'd finally begin talking seriously about marriage?

He wanted to go see her but wasn't sure if it was an appropriate time. The mansion would be busy right now with the coffin being laid out for the wake, relatives and well-wishers stopping by, and helpers preparing food for the reception after the church funeral.

He was in the process of rolling a cigarette when the door opened up and Ab Soames stuck his head in.

"Just wanted you to know that I haven't forgotten you, Sheriff."

"Feel good to be out of jail?"

"Believe it or not, I've lived in worse places."

"You staying sober?"

"That's why I'm wondering if I could stay here tonight."

"In jail?"

"Be obliged if I could. I'm still workin' on that memory of mine. Man I seen runnin' out of my uncle's den that night he was murdered."

"Think we've already got our man, Ab. Told you that when I let you out of your cell."

"Yeah, I know." He smiled. "What I really want is someplace to stay. I think you got your man, too—you know who he is, anyway—but I ain't got no money and if I go see a couple ole friends of mine, I'll start drinkin' sure enough."

"Sure thing, Ab."

He came in and closed the door. "Poor Annie. She's such a nice gal."

"She sure is."

"You just never know how somebody's gonna turn out." Then he snorted. "Guess that's what most of my relatives say about me. 'Just never know how somebody's gonna turn out.'"

FOUR

MATTHEWS WAS ABOUT a block from his office when Roy Fuller said hello. He'd just finished locking the door to the Davies office and appeared to be headed home himself.

"Any luck with that Reynolds fella yet?" Fuller asked.

"Not yet."

"Well, at least you know who you're looking for now. Just wish we'd have known before Mr. Davies was killed." He made an unhappy sound with his mouth. "That's where I'm headed right now, in fact. Pay my respects to Karen."

"We're headed the same place then."

The dying day always made Matthews melancholy. Something about the layers of gold and salmon pink and flame blue, something about the rising moon and the sinking sun, a purgatory that was not quite night and not quite day. Even having some drinks, even surrounded by jolly people he liked, he couldn't look long at a sunset without feeling the temporary, fleeting, futile sense of life—a million million sunsets since the dawn of time (that's what those smart people in *Harper's Magazine* had claimed lately, anyway)—and all trace of those who'd gone before lost in the mindless march of day into night into day. He hated thoughts like these. He wanted to cling to the religion all those around him seemed to believe in without question. But somehow at moments like these, religion wasn't enough, and he cursed his lack of faith. Lucky is the man who believes without doubt. He had no idea what any of this meant exactly, or why he'd felt it since his earliest teen years. He just wished he didn't have to endure it every time a sunset began to paint itself across the sky.

"He was a good man," Fuller said.

"What?" He had the sense that Fuller had been talking all along. He hadn't heard a word.

"Mr. Davies."

"Oh. Yes. He was."

"He had his faults."

"I suppose he did."

"But then we all do."

"Can't argue there," Matthews responded with a minimum of words. The damned sunset still gripped him, that odd crazy sorrow he experienced a couple of times a month. But then, in the graying light, he saw the magnificent Davies house, lights even more brilliant than the lazy moon, buggies and chevrons and hansoms lining the edge of the limitless green lawn, and people in their finest strolling toward the vast open porch as if this was a party and not a wake.

His mood changed abruptly. To hell with the sunset. All this human spectacle and noise banished his melancholy. He was once again—happily, comfortably—part of the pack and not some isolated figure with treasonous thoughts.

A chandelier in the large open area sprawling before the grand staircase cast sparkling light on the faces of some of the most important people in the entire valley. The conversations were subdued and ran mostly to laments about Vernon Davies. Afterward, after a few prayers and some words spoken by a minister, then they would feel bold enough to talk of other things.

Matthews attracted more attention than he wanted to. His presence seemed to please some—some folks just naturally felt more comfortable when some kind of official authority was present—while others seemed to see him as a vulgar reminder that a murder had intruded on their lives . . . a lawman not being in their social circle, after all.

He was uncomfortable as he stood in front of the closed coffin and said a prayer. He wasn't good at prayers. He had a lot of religious thoughts—his own kind of religion, anyway—but they never exactly formed into what you'd call a prayer.

When he was finished, and turned back to the crowded parlor that was now packed with people, he saw Karen for the first time tonight. She was radiant in her grief, in the black dress, in the sooted look of the flesh below her eyes, in the uneasy elegance of her gestures. He wanted to protect her, hold her, say something comforting.

She stood in a circle of people who were trying to give her the same sort of comfort Matthews had in mind. He recognized a few of them as relatives. She had that gallant look women took on in moments of grief. You could see how hard they struggled to forgo tears and that made them seem all the more gallant. She glanced once at him, offering him a tiny smile that he wasn't sure was a smile at all.

The best thing you could say about the braying peacock of a minister—known as the most interminable preacher in the valley—was that he was loud. He was one of those men who reduced the entire world to himself. If he ever spoke about Lincoln or Grant, it wouldn't be to talk about them or their accomplishments. It would be about how he'd known them. And thus the subject was really himself as always.

He treated Vernon Davies no differently. According to how he contrived his little sermon, Davies hadn't had much of a life outside of knowing the minister here. And several of the charitable ideas that Davies had taken credit for? Well, according to the minister, they were all his. And Davies's vague hope of running for elective office someday? Once again, the idea had been the minister's. And not because he was so high on Davies per se, but simply because "my job as God's messenger is to see that our legislature is filled with men who do right by the Bible and right by their Lord. These men seek me out for wisdom and succor and I am most happy — as God's messenger — to give it to them."

Matthews stayed in the back so he could leave early. He stood on the sweeping porch, rolling a cigarette, feeling the cold bite of impending rain on the night air.

He had just taken his first drag on the cigarette when a slim arm slid through his. "What an ass he is."

"Gosh," Matthews said, "I hadn't noticed."

At first, Karen obviously didn't realize he was joking. Then she jabbed him playfully in the ribs. "You didn't think it was a bit much when he took credit for building the pyramids?"

"No. But I was surprised when he said that he gave Washington some advice on winning the Revolutionary War."

She laughed. "I know I should be mourning and it's probably terrible to be this silly — but I need it right now. It's been a long day."

"You moved fast."

"That's how Dad wanted it. Wake the same day if possible; funeral the next morning. You know how much he hated ceremonies. I guess he thought that if I had to move fast, I wouldn't have time to 'gussy it all up' as he liked to say." She put her head to his shoulder. "I miss him."

He slid his arm around her. Let her cry gently. "I didn't know people could cry this much," she said.

"You didn't seem to be doing much of it this morning. You need to do it now."

"I hate crying in front of other people, though. It's embarrassing. If I start crying when that blowhard gets through in there, hit me, will you?"

"I'd rather kick you."

"All right." She smiled. "You can kick me if you don't kick too hard."

"No broken bones, I promise."

She jabbed him again the girlish way she had before. He loved it when she did things like that.

They stood off to the west side of the front doors. Bryce Harlow and Hector Nolan came rushing out of those doors. Hector was glancing at his vest watch. They looked stern, worried. They didn't glance around. They walked straight for Harlow's buggy. They obviously had somewhere to go and needed to get there fast.

"I think I'll see where they're going," Matthews said.

"They probably couldn't take any more of the minister."

"I've been trying to find them all day, anyway."

"For what?"

"I need to know how many times they heard from Paul Reynolds. And how they left it with him. Maybe they can help me."

"You think they'll be prosecuted?"

"Hard to say. I haven't really told anybody *why* this Reynolds has been killing people. Just that we need to stop him. I'm guessing that Harlow and Nolan think their secret is still safe."

"That they raped that girl." She hesitated. "And by 'they,' I mean my dad, too?"

He nodded. "They're probably still hoping that the whole story can still be kept a secret. They can probably explain that this Paul Reynolds wanted to kill them because of some business deal. It's all going to be up to Annie Reynolds. How much she wants to tell. There're some legal issues, too, such as a statute of limitations. But I haven't told anybody about why her brother came out here and I doubt she has, either. At this point, it's up to her. All the town knows is that her brother is a killer."

"I feel sorry for her."

"So do I. I guess her brother hasn't been very stable his whole life. They grew up in pretty bad circumstances. Her brother always watched out for the little sister while Annie worked. The mother died when they were young and the father drifted off someplace. He was a drunk."

He watched as Harlow and Nolan climbed into the buggy. Harlow took the reins and smartly eased the vehicle out of its slot along the edge of the lawn. Night had blackened the sky; starlight shone like a celestial version of the mansion's chandelier.

Matthews kissed her on the cheek. "I'll talk to you tomorrow after the funeral."

She slid her hand in his. "We have a lot to talk about."

"I know."

"But I can't make any promises. You know, about our—future."

He nodded.

"You still scare me, Reed. I can't help it. My first marriage—"

"I'll talk to you tomorrow."

And then he was off. He had no idea where Harlow and Nolan were leading him. And it didn't matter. Matthews's instincts were operating again. He knew Harlow and Nolan were going to take him somewhere very interesting.

FIVE

THERE WAS AN old timber road that wound up through acres of pine that had never been cleared. That was work for the next generation, as the farmers liked to say.

The road was dusty and treacherous because of all the holes in it. Harlow drove his buggy recklessly. Certainly, as somebody who'd lived here a long time, he had to know how dangerous this road could be. But he didn't slow down for any of the curves nor for any of the especially bad patches of ruts and holes that had snapped many an axle in two.

Matthews didn't worry about them spotting him. He kept a quarter mile behind and stayed in the shadows of the looming trees whenever possible. The air was fresh, moonlight glazed everything, and an assortment of creatures filled the night with eerie but lovely music. Every once in a while, he'd see three or four pairs of raccoon eyes burning in the gloom of the thick branches. A couple times deer appeared at the side of the road to watch him—all beautiful anxiety, these most elegant and deft of God's earthly family—only to leap away as he drew nearer.

He had to give Harlow one thing. He was the most unrelenting sonofabitch Matthews had ever seen on a road like this one. Several times, the buggy hit a rut so deep and wide, the vehicle was tossed up in the air, a foot or two between the road and the bottom of the wheels. But he never slowed down.

Matthews began to smell the river. The bluffs above the water were a familiar rendezvous spot for valley people. Adulterers, family picnickers, bird watchers, city folks who liked to hike—the bluffs had something for everybody.

In the night, the area where the buggy stopped was dark thanks to the surrounding forest of pines. Harlow pulled the buggy in so close to the tree line that it virtually disappeared in the gloom.

Matthews ground-tied his horse and worked his way toward the wagon through the dense shadow-laden, pine-smelling darkness of the forest.

Pine branches whipped at him. The soles of his boots got sticky from pine blood. He followed a path that ended, and then had to take to underbrush that clawed at him like pincers. For a time, the voices of Harlow and Nolan got, if anything, fainter and fainter. A trailsman he was not, he thought.

To his right, distant as the voices, he heard the sounds

of crackling undergrowth. Somebody else making his way through another section of undergrowth. Either that or an animal so big, Matthews didn't want to think about it.

Somebody else out here.

Matthews stopped moving, listened. The undergrowth continued to part noisily. This new man wasn't a trailsman, either. He seemed as lost as Matthews.

Gradually, the sounds of brush, twigs, and bushes being parted and stepped on, stopped. Or maybe the man had just moved out of hearing range.

Matthews stood gleaming inside a shell of hot, gluey sweat. Was it safe for him to move again? He didn't want to be detected. But if he didn't move, he knew he was going to miss what was so obviously a rendezvous— Harlow and Nolan and whoever this stranger was.

Matthews was already forming an idea of what was going on here. He had the sense that if he was smart and quick, he'd soon have Paul Reynolds in custody and soon have a confession from Harlow and Nolan. From there, as he'd told Karen, it would be left to Annie Reynolds to press charges or not.

He moved. Tiny, cautious steps at first as he made his agonized way through bramble that he hoped would lead him to a narrow path he thought he'd glimpsed a few minutes ago. This damned forest, he'd decided, was a dead end of crisscrossing paths it would take an Indian scout or a mountain man to navigate.

Then it happened.

The damnedest thing of all.

He'd just picked up the sound of the stranger again

working his way through the underbrush—presumably toward Harlow and Nolan—when he heard the buggy start to move.

Where the hell were they going? Hadn't they had a rendezvous set up with this stranger? And what was the stranger thinking now that he heard the buggy pulling away?

Then Matthews realized he was being stupid. Not thinking clearly.

What the two men were doing was leaving blackmail money for Paul Reynolds to pick up. He would likely have instructed them to drop the money off and leave. And they were just following instructions.

Matthews hurried. The narrow path was just where he'd hoped it would be. He noticed immediately that the noises from the underbrush had ceased. Either the man had frozen in place because of the buggy leaving. Or he'd gotten to his destination and was now just waiting for the buggy to vanish from sight so he could collect his money.

Matthews reached the tree line, crouched down, and looked out at the grassy clearing that ran along the bluff. He could hear and smell the river below. The wind off it dried his sweat, balmed him. He closed his eyes, letting his enjoyment of it be full and rich.

He didn't have to worry about missing any action. Because for five full minutes nothing happened. He couldn't even hear a forest creature making any noise. There was just the soughing wind and the lapping water on the narrow beach below.

Then the man made his move.

In the center of the clearing, Harlow and Nolan had left a black leather bag such as a doctor carried. Moonlight traced it, lent it the importance it deserved. A naked lady holding two flaming torches couldn't have been more conspicuous than that black bag was at the moment. The entire universe was focused on that bag.

The man made his move.

And so did Harlow and Nolan.

What they did in principle made sense. But what they did in reality was stupid. The idea was to hide in the trees on the far side of the clearing and then shoot the blackmailer as he approached the black bag. Good, sound idea for getting rid of a parasite who was going to bleed you for the rest of your life.

But they were too anxious.

They barely let the man get a foot or so from his hiding place on his own side of the clearing when they opened fire.

Just as Matthews was no trailsman, Harlow and Nolan were no crack shots. They didn't come close to hitting him. What they did do, though, was frighten him away. He dove back into the shadows of the forest and began charging down the path he'd used to get here.

Matthews knew it would be simpler to run out into the clearing, race down the grass, and then plunge into the trees at about the same point the blackmailer had.

Which is what he'd done when he saw Harlow and Nolan, rifles ready, charging across the clearing and firing at him. They obviously couldn't see who he was. He had the sense they wouldn't have cared who he was, anyway. They were frustrated that they'd missed their man first time through, and now would settle for shooting anybody they could get in their sights. They were like drunken posse members who shot up cows if they couldn't find anything else to empty their guns into.

The only thing Matthews could do was forget about the blackmailer and throw himself to the ground before Harlow and Nolan killed him. He hit the ground rolling, shouting for them to stop firing. There was a great temptation to start firing back at them. He resisted it.

It took a few more minutes before they figured out why he was shouting and who he was. They were practically on top of him before Harlow said, "It's the sheriff!"

"Well, I'll be damned," Nolan said. "He must be the blackmailer."

Confronted with such massive brainpower, all Matthews could do was jump to his feet and say, "I must be the blackmailer? You stupid bastards scared him away. We could've caught him."

"Oh," Nolan said, still not getting it. "When I saw you, I figured you must be his accomplice."

Harlow finally comprehended. "What'd you do, follow us?"

"Yeah. Followed you. Hid in the woods. Waited to see what you'd do. After you left, I was getting ready to sneak up on him. Then you came back and started shooting."

"Oh," Nolan said, as if he'd just discovered the way to turn brass into gold, "I get it now." Nolan was living proof you didn't need to be smart to get rich. You needed a little bit of cunning, but more than anything else you needed luck. Just plain old luck.

"You think he's gone?" Harlow said.

"The head start he's got? Sure, he's gone."

"I'm sorry, Sheriff," Harlow said.

"Me, too, Sheriff."

Matthews sighed. "You'll hear from him again."

"Yeah," Harlow said, looking at the black bag several feet from where he stood. "The money."

"The money," Matthews said. "And then he'll be gone. That's why I need you to tell me when you hear from him—right away. I need to be there when he picks up the money."

"You don't have to worry about that," Nolan said. "We'll help you every way we can."

Yeah, Matthews thought, *that's what I'm afraid of. You'll help me just the way you did when you scared him off.*

A silence, followed by Harlow saying: "I suppose you want to know what happened back then. Why he's blackmailing us."

"Annie already told me."

"Oh."

"We're in trouble," Nolan said.

"You weren't very damned smart. You should've gone to the law right where you were."

"We wanted to, Sheriff," Nolan said, "but Vernon wouldn't let us."

"Damnit, Nolan," Harlow said. "Don't start lying about our friends. We took a vote and every single one of us voted against going to the law."

"Well, I wanted to go but I finally gave in to the rest of you fellas."

"That's another lie," Harlow said.

They stood in the clearing, the wind coming up off the river clean and cool and good. For just a second there, Matthews let nature overwhelm him, the scents of the forest, the silver sustenance of moonlight, the sweet soughing sounds of the knee-length grass. For just that moment all human problems seemed wind-banished and he was nurtured by the earth—soil and water and blooming things—and in that instant he forgot all the griefs of the planet and just exalted in the natural pleasures surrounding him.

And then Nolan had to go and spoil it by saying: "I hope you kill him when you catch him. He's got no right to do this to us."

"Harlow, will you please explain to your friend here what you did to his sister?"

"We killed her, Nolan. We killed his sister."

"We didn't mean to."

"We didn't mean to but she wouldn't have died if we hadn't done what we'd done."

"She was a whore. She should've been used to being raped. Anyway, I'm not sure you can rape a whore. Technically speaking."

"Nolan," Matthews said evenly. "Try and understand this. It doesn't matter that she was a whore. It doesn't matter that you didn't mean to kill her. Not to him, it doesn't. To him, you had a hand in killing her, whether you planned it or not. That's all he knows and all he cares about. That's why he's killing you. He's just doing what he thinks is right."

"You sound like you're defending him, Sheriff," Nolan said.

"You keep accusing me of things, Nolan, and you're going to piss me off. First you had me being his accomplice. Now I'm defending him?"

"Just shut up, Nolan," Harlow said. "You're a horse's ass and everybody knows it."

"Yeah, well, you want to hear what everybody knows about you, Harlow? Mr. Goody Two-Shoes sneakin' off to see that Mexican woman down by Archer Creek."

"Enough." Matthews said it harshly enough that they both heeded him. "This is getting useless. Now, you both know what I expect from you. The minute he drops a note off saying where he wants to meet you next time, you let me know. I want to be there. And if you let me down, either one of you, there's gonna be hell to pay. You understand?"

They nodded.

"Now go over there and pick up your bag and clear the hell out of here."

They'd given up resisting. Just easier to go along. The evening had divided them. They'd never be friends again. Matthews didn't give a damn. He didn't like either of them, anyway.

He went back to town, to his office, to see if anything important had happened while he'd been gone. It hadn't.

SIX

"D ID YOU EVER think you might get a disease?"
Azalea Nolan said to the man next to her in bed.
That was how she felt about him, now that he'd explained what had been going on. The man. Not her husband. Some stranger.

"I guess I didn't consider that."

She was having her way tonight. Normally, he rubbed
his liniment on before going to bed, a smell she loathed.
But she usually had to go along with him. Not tonight.
She'd told him not to put it on and he damned well hadn't.

Same with the cat Princess. Since their children had
grown and gone, Princess had become an ersatz daughter to Azalea. She wanted the tawny Princess to sleep
with them, but her husband had always said no. He didn't
say no tonight. Princess slept on Azalea's chest tonight.

"I'm not sure I ever want you to touch me again."

"Oh, you don't mean that."

"Don't I?"

"Fellas make mistakes all the time."

"You're not a 'fella.' "

"Sure, I'm a fella. What else would I be?"

"You're my husband is what you are."

"Well, I'm still a fella."

She stroked the cat's head. "I wish everybody could be as good as you are, Princess. You'd never go off and do anything naughty, would you, darling?"

And what made it worse was that she was talking baby talk to Princess.

You always heard jokes about sleeping on the couch. Until tonight, Harlow had never had that particular experience. He was too long for the couch, for one thing. And he couldn't roll over, for another. He'd tried it and when he did so, facing the back of the couch, his ass hung over the edge. How could a man sleep with his ass hanging off the couch and when he had to scrunch up his legs on top of it?

There was only one person more religious—to say sanctimonious—than Bryce Harlow in the Harlow household, and that was Stella Harlow.

He'd tried three times to get into the bedroom to apologize again. He wouldn't have told her about the whole thing except he knew that the story would be all over town by morning and he wanted to break the news to her in his own particular way. He'd been a little high-handed about it. He'd said, "We all had a little too much to drink and this girl was there and—"

Then his wife had stopped him. "This girl was there? She just magically appeared?"

"Well, somebody—probably Vernon, his wife being dead and all—I guess Vernon probably invited her when we were in the saloon where she worked."

"And then you all got drunk and—"

"She—well, she started crying."

"Crying? You had a whore who was crying? I didn't know that whores were *supposed* to cry. Not unless you *pay* them to cry. What was she crying *about*?"

"Oh, you know, that she'd ruined her life by being a whore and that she was going to give Vernon his money back and just leave and—"

"I wonder what the people at church will make of all this."

"Let's not talk about that right now."

"Let's *do* talk about it. Everybody thinks you're so holy and good and—just wait till they hear about this. As a Christian gentleman, you should've *encouraged* that girl to leave."

"I know, I know. God, do I know."

"So you four made her stay there—"

"I didn't ask her to stay. At least I can say that much for myself."

"And she tried to leave and—"

"They stopped her. The others. And she wouldn't do—anything—just threw the money on the floor and tried to get out the door and they dragged her back and—"

"—raped her."

"Yes."

"And you raped her, too."

He said nothing.

"And you raped her, too."

"Yes."

"She was crying, asking for Christian help, and you—"

So here he was sleeping on the couch. With his ass hanging off.

Lord God, he couldn't believe he'd actually raped that girl when she'd been struggling, fighting, sobbing. He'd always considered himself such a good man, such a cut above when you came right down to it. A good and decent and exemplary man and—

—and here he was sleeping on the couch.

Annie Reynolds believed that if you wished for something and then put it out of your mind, it would happen. If you thought about it, it would *never* happen. The trouble was, how could you *not* think about what she was trying not to think about?

She worked, figuring that if she stayed up all night and made candles, absorbed in her work rather than thinking about what she shouldn't think about— maybe it would happen.

Maybe Paul would knock on her door and she would feed him and hold him and then when day broke, she would take him to see Reed Matthews. She would also get the best lawyer she could afford. She would tell the lawyer everything that happened the night her little sister was raped by the four men. How she cried and pleaded to be let go. How she'd become sick of her life. How she'd even thrown the money back at them. *Just*

please let me go, that's all I ask, just please let me go.
Annie was like Paul in that respect, spent a lot of time—
ever since the witness revealed what had happened—
playing those words over and over in her mind, trying to
imagine how terrifying it must have been to have four
seemingly respectable men turn on you like that.

A jury who heard about that night would certainly
take pity on Paul. Especially when this was paired with
stories of Paul's troubles all his life. Of not being quite
right. Of being treated so bad in that hospital. Of suffering over his dead sister.

Reed Matthews might have some ideas. He was a fair
man. He might even help her find the right lawyer.

She'd tried to sleep earlier but it had been no use. She
just kept seeing the same pictures in her mind. The posse
finding Paul. Capturing him as if he were an animal.
Throwing their ropes around him. Dragging him. Laughing at his cries. Oh, he would come apart. She could hear
him screaming, pleading for their mercy. But unless
Reed was there to control them, there would be no
mercy. Paul might well be dead by the time they got him
back to town.

Now, she sipped coffee and stared at the door. Just
couldn't help herself. Had to imagine him there in the
doorway. They wouldn't argue this time. She'd see to
that.

But no matter how hard she stared at the door, he
didn't appear.

She was barely aware of the tears burning her cheeks
as she went about dipping some new wicks into the tallow. She'd cried so often tonight that she'd become ac-

customed to the feel and faint scent of tears. She'd done this so many times when he was a boy and they were trying to survive the slums of Chicago. When he'd come home sobbing because somebody had called him a particularly vile name—or because somebody had beaten him up—or because that especially mean girl down the block had played another one of her callous practical jokes on him, delighting the audience of kids who were hiding behind trees, doors, and stoops to witness Paul making a fool of himself again.

His pain had always been hers. Just as their little sister's pain had always been Paul's. She'd never even minded that Paul loved the little one more than he loved Annie.

Skilled as she was, her preoccupation led her to dip her fingers into the hot tallow and burn herself badly. She barely noticed it.

SEVEN

O N THE WAY to work, Matthews stopped at the house that was being used as a hospital until the real thing could be built.

The nurse in charge told him it would be all right to bring Harold Lincoln a cup of coffee from the kitchen. Harold sat up in bed in the small, bright room. Two wooden chairs were pulled up near the head of the bed. Visitors. The smell of various medicines was reassuring. Something was being done, and done well, for one of the men he admired most. That was the message the medicinal odors sent Matthews. These were the official smells of getting well. They were, at any rate, to a man who didn't know jack shit about medicine.

The fierce morning sunlight showed just how pale Harold was. Matthews had never noticed before how lined Harold's face was and how old the blue eyes could seem. There was suddenly a sense of vulnerability and mortality in the room—not just Harold's, not just his own, but that of the entire species. Human beings were born to die. It was that simple and that sorry a state of affairs.

"I feel better than I look," Harold said. He seemed to know what Matthews was thinking.

"You look fine."

"Now when you hand me a pile of bullshit like that, do you get paid by the pound?"

Matthews laughed. "You don't look bad, put it that way."

"I was lucky." He took the coffee and sipped it. "This isn't a whole hell of a lot better than what we have at the office."

"If I had any rye on me, I'd slip you a little."

"That's all right. I already saw my wife and my daughter this morning. A little bit of bad coffee isn't going to ruin my day. Not after the way they were smiling." He winked. "They seem to be under the impression that I'm going to get out of this bed someday and walk home all on my own and be just fine."

He was cranked up in the medical bed. But after speaking just those few words, he sighed deeply and put his head back against the pillow. This was the moment he couldn't cajole his way around. He had a long way to go before complete recovery, tired as he got just talking.

When he closed his eyes, it was all too easy to imagine him a corpse in a coffin. Matthews was happy when his old friend opened those blue eyes again.

"You going out with this posse again?"

Matthews nodded. "We meet in another half hour."

"Annie could be hidin' him, much as I hate to say it."

"I've got Bill Pearson watching her place."

Harold laughed and then coughed up phlegm. "He bring his granddad's musket, did he?"

There was a group of auxiliary deputies. Half of them just wanted to lend a civic hand. Matthews appreciated them. The other half were grown-up children who wanted to play deputy. They were sort of sad to Matthews, living out their boyhood dreams so publicly. Bill Pearson's only weapon was his granddad's old musket. He had a handgun somewhere but never could seem to find it. So he toted that musket around. Matthews and Harold both assumed the thing would blow up in Pearson's hands if he ever actually fired it.

"Say, that new Pinkerton man stopped in last night. Seems like a nice fella."

"Yeah," Matthews said. "He want anything special?"

"Just asked if I'd ever talked to Carney about what he was doing here. I told him no."

The coughing started quick and deadly as a gunshot. Here was pale Harold lying back with his eyes at half-mast, lying quiet and still, and then he was bouncing on the bed, he was hacking with such violence.

The nurse came dashing in, brushing past Matthews to pour a glass of water, gently pushed Harold back on his bed, and forced some water down his throat.

Matthews waited until he was sure Harold was all right, then—the nurse looking appreciative—he said good-bye and walked back to the office.

• • •

Matthews didn't go out with the posse. He had to testify
in a rustling trial. One ranch owner accused another of
stealing cattle from yet another ranch owner. The defendant claimed that the cattle had "wandered" onto his
property. The owner making the charges had his lawyer
say that he had a "witness" to the rustling. The witness
turned out to be the owner's own somewhat disreputable
brother-in-law, who had a glass eye, a gold tooth, and a
grin as cold as the grave. Matthews had been subpoe-
naed to testify because he'd seen the defendant drunkenly swing on his accuser one night in a saloon. The
accuser's lawyer insisted that this was proof positive that
the accused was guilty. Even the judge, usually the most
professional of jurists, dozed through part of this one.
Neither man presented an especially believable case.
Matthews guessed that the defendant would be found
innocent because of the brother-in-law, who used that
icy, predatory grin way too much during his time in the
witness chair. The glass eye didn't help, either. It was
ridiculous, it was prejudicial, it was all kinds of horse-
shit things, but there you had it. Juries would decide
cases for reasons they would be ashamed to admit out
loud. The defendant walked free.

Matthews hated going to court.

Annie Reynolds walked through the front door about
noon. There was nobody up front so she walked on back
and knocked on Matthews's office door.

He knew right away by the way her shoulders
slumped that her brother hadn't come to her. She looked

drained. She leaned against the door frame. He half-expected her to slide down it.

"You know what I'm afraid of? That one of those jackasses of yours'll find him and kill him on the spot."

"You want some coffee?"

"You didn't answer my question."

"You didn't *ask* me a question."

"I sure as hell did."

"You *told* me that one of my so-called jackasses would find him and kill him on the spot. That isn't a question. That's a statement."

"It's the same thing."

He sighed. "Look. You're frustrated and scared and you want to pick a fight. But we both want the same thing here, Annie. You want your brother and so do I."

"Yeah, but you want him dead."

"I'd prefer him alive. Think about it, Annie. You've been here long enough. How many men have I shot? One? Two? And I've never *killed* anybody."

"Your men might."

"You want some coffee?"

"There you go again. You didn't answer my question."

He stood up and walked around his desk and went over to her and took her in his arms and held her. She was a small woman. She didn't resist. She cried and he let her cry and when she was almost done crying, he led her over to one of the chairs in front of the desk and then he went and got her some coffee.

When he was seated again, he said, "You have any idea where he could be hiding?"

"Someplace high. That's how he was when we were

growing up. He always found the highest place he could to hide. He usually went to roofs."

"The highest point would be that old deserted cabin on Leaning Rock."

"You still never answered my question about your posse killing him."

"I gave them orders to bring him in alive. I figure they'll do that unless their lives are at stake."

"You trust them?"

He looked at her. Decided not to lie. "Not every one of them, no. But I tried to pair them off in such a way that I have a very responsible man partnered up with a man I have doubts about. I figure that's the best way to handle it."

"They could still kill him."

He took his time before speaking. "Annie, your brother has killed three men. There's only so much any lawman can guarantee in bringing in a man like that."

She took his words without any expression of anger. "I suppose you're right."

"Have you checked on that cabin? It's right on the edge of town."

There were times when you needed to take action even if you realized in advance that the action would be futile. Action as a way of doing something rather than just sitting still and driving yourself and everybody around you crazy.

This was one of those times. She needed to *do* something, anything that broke the choke hold of fear and misery that paralyzed her.

"Let's go out to Leaning Rock," he said.

Leaning Rock was a vast, shelflike boulder that could have supported three cabins if it had needed to. One of the town founders, a man who'd been Amish until he was thirty and who was then set upon by greed, had come out here from Iowa determined to become rich. And he did become rich. Once. And briefly. He took his fortune to Denver and lost it at a crap table after—he realized later—being drugged and cheated by two cardsharps. He looked them up the morning after and killed them in their hotel beds. Then he came back to town here, to the somewhat patchwork cabin he'd originally built himself on Leaning Rock, put a pistol barrel in his mouth, and got himself pretty much picked to the bone before anybody found him.

Given his sudden bad luck, locals, illogically enough, began to believe that the cabin on the rock was evil and should be avoided. And even a skeptic had to admit that the few people who'd inhabited it since then had come to strange and sad ends. It could all be explained rationally, but rational stories like that make for piss-poor campfire tales. Better you have some cosmic demon at work. That's the sort of thing you need for the kind of campfire stories that get told again and again.

No sign of life whatsoever. The lone door shut, no recent road apples, not even a scrap of paper blowing in the hot gritty wind you got nine months of the year up here on this wide exposed shelf of rock. The cabin had been built on soil, of course, but it abutted the rock exactly.

And from it—standing in front of the cabin—you had a godlike view of the town spread below in the timber- and river-rich valley. Handsome farms and roads, gleaming railroad tracks that'd take you all the way to heaven if you had the money, and a town of new buildings that boasted of ingenuity and prosperity. God had blessed the town because the townspeople had blessed themselves with hard work and honest hearts and a genuine desire to make life even better for the children just now coming up.

"You don't see the truth from up here," she said in the boiling day.

"What truth's that?"

"Oh, how people really are. In their hearts, I mean."

"Pretty good bunch of people here, I'd say."

"They're going to kill my brother."

She had exchanged anger for grief. Matthews would have been the same way. Blood kin of his being hunted. Would have blamed the people for wanting justice.

He was going to argue with her, but what was the point?

"You want to go in and look around?"

She shrugged. "Guess we might as well."

One room. You couldn't walk two inches without stepping on hard, dry turds of various kinds. The cabin was in so much disrepair that the rats had eaten away a good deal of the lone mattress and the faded red blanket that covered it. Everything stank of decay. The dirt floor smelled the way old graves did. Broken glasses and plates were strewn everywhere. One wall was a mosaic of bullet holes. Kids taking target practice, no doubt. Dusty sunlight streamed through the neat little holes.

She said, "He was here." She held up a newspaper. Chicago. Three weeks ago.

"Yeah," he said, "he was here, all right."

"Maybe he's hiding in the woods to the west. Maybe he just comes back here at night." She looked at the front page of the newspaper. "He hates Chicago. But he always ends up going back there."

"Let's take a walk over to those woods."

She walked over to him, letting the newspaper fall to the floor. She grasped his forearm. "I never thought about it before."

"Thought about what?"

"What I'll say to him when I see him. I want to tell him to run but—" She still clutched his arm. "I don't suppose that's the right thing to say to a lawman, is it? Telling him to run."

"Let's see if we can find him first. Then you can worry about what to say to him."

When he reconstructed it later, how somebody could get away with something like this, Nolan figured it must have happened this way: Nolan's office was in the back of the building, close enough to the rear door that he could scurry home without having to walk past his employees who always gave him a smirk because they knew what he knew in his heart—that he was a slacker. Of his group of rich men, he was the only one who'd come from money, and had thus had considerable financial help to get going in both his businesses, steamboats and dry goods, the latter of which, with the coming of the railroads, solidified his fortune. But the staff knew the secret. He hired the right people and they made the right decisions and when they wanted their fair share for making him wealthy, he fired them and hired younger right people. Nolan was unaware of the daily office pool—what time the old man would sneak out the back door today.

But this matter wasn't about sneaking out. This matter was about sneaking in.

Half an hour ago, Nolan had gone up front to where the secretaries were. He liked to flirt with them, creaky and awkward as he was. Long ago a girl—wanting a job—had told him in her best contrived blushing manner that Nolan looked just like her uncle, "the one all the ladies make such a fuss over." Nolan never forgot that. And so, despite all the evidence to the contrary—jowls, unwholesome-looking teeth, a whiskey nose, and too-dry eyes that were forever blinking—he imagined that the secretaries all liked it when he came up front to flirt. The kindest of them—the few that didn't smirk—saw it all as sad, a rich ugly old man being very, very foolish.

But . . . the back door.

Though it was locked, somebody had managed to *un*-lock it and sneak inside long enough to leave an envelope on Nolan's desk.

When he returned from giving the ladies their thrill for the day, he saw the envelope and knew exactly what it was. Didn't need to open it. Didn't need to weigh it on the palm of his hand. Didn't even need to *touch* it. Just knew exactly what it was.

The back-door ploy bothered him more than the envelope did. Nolan had built his entire insecure life on being as invulnerable as possible. If you wanted to fuck with him, you paid a price. And fucking with him was not an easy thing to do. He was a believer in locks, body-guards when necessary, sentries if it came to that.

So he goes up front for a little harmless flirting and he finds this envelope on his desk. Somebody having snuck in his back door. His *locked* back door.

Sonofabitch; sonofabitch.

Bryce Harlow had a slightly different experience.

Just before noon—which was to be a Rotary lunch-eon at which a so-called "white Indian" was to talk about how he'd personally scalped more than three hundred Apaches in Arizona—Harlow concluded a staff meeting he'd been having for the past two hours (he graded staff meetings not by accomplishment but by duration) and then went up front to collect his suit coat from the coat tree just inside the reception area.

He didn't notice it at first.

He had taken exactly five steps on the sidewalk when he felt it. He stopped. Instinct told him what it was.

He stalked back to his office, stood in a confronta-tional way in front of Mrs. Carmichael's reception desk, and said, "Somebody put an envelope in my suit jacket this morning, Mrs. Carmichael. I want to know who it was."

Mrs. Carmichael was a competent, aloof woman who had learned long ago that the best way to deal with Har-low was to treat him just as he treated you. If he was pleasant, she was pleasant; if he was angry, as now, she was angry.

"We were very busy this morning. Very busy. People in and out. So many people at one point that there weren't enough chairs for everybody. If somebody slipped something into your coat, I didn't see it."

He noted that she offered no apology, merely an icy explanation.

He hadn't opened the envelope yet. Didn't need to.

He had to give Paul Reynolds his cunning. Walk right into a man's office—most likely in disguise—and slip your blackmail demand right into his suit coat. The man had brass. You had to give him that.

"I'll be at lunch," he said.

She just gave him one of her Mrs. Carmichael looks. The kind that secretly scared the hell out of him and made him feel a whole lot less than manly. He was the boss. It said so on his letterhead and business card, didn't it?

Miserable, shaken, he left to hear a presentation about scalping by some huckster who earned a living conning service organizations out of their speakers-bureau money.

He prayed to God that Nolan would be there. He needed desperately to talk to Nolan and see if he, too, had gotten an envelope.

They spent an hour in the forest and found nothing. This tract was a mix of hardwoods and jack pines. Recent rains had created tiny pools so sensitive to intrusion that a fly settling on one could break the surface into circles.

The scent of wet foliage combined with loam to create a heady aroma that was somehow ancient.

Sometimes Annie cried in seizurelike spasms. She no longer wanted to be held. She pushed back any attempts to touch her.

"He imagines things," she said at one point, "thinks they're real when they aren't. That's why they put him away that time. It was so terrible for him. I told you that." She sat on a fallen tree as she said this. "Maybe he didn't kill them."

"Maybe not."

"You don't believe it, do you, you fucker?"

"I'd like to believe it, Annie. I really would."

"You'd kill him yourself if you got half a chance, wouldn't you?"

The immemorial forest. The sanctity of it. Every once in a while he'd hear mothers telling their kids animal stories. He'd always loved animal stories. Dogs and cats that talked. Owls that were so wise. Pigs that danced. Birds so big and strong you could fly on their backs if they were in the right mood. To imagine that there was a better world nearby where you could escape to. Live with rabbits and raccoons and deer for a while. Let them show you their world.

But moments like these spoiled the forest for him. Because her grief was so overwhelming, there was no hope of whimsy. Of fantasy. He watched that sweet little face become filthy with inconsolable pain. Somebody'd find Paul and maybe they would kill him. Even worse, they'd find him and they *wouldn't* kill him. And then there'd be a trial. And then there'd be a sentence. And she would be able to think of nothing but her brother. She would have her lawyer frantically file petitions. She would verbally attack judges. She would visit Paul again and again in the damp stone prison, barely able to keep from breaking down in front of him. And then execution day would come and there she'd be, weighing ten pounds less than she did now, gray of skin, gaunt like a cancer patient, a madness now indelibly tainting those once-lucid brown eyes. She wouldn't scream the way some of them did, not when they slipped the hood over his head, not when they cinched the hangman's knot around his neck, not when the executioner opened the chute delivering Paul unto death. And she would die with him. People said that all the time. That so-and-so died when his wife did. And that was a true human thing. It happened to people. They might have a pulse, they might even be known to laugh once in a while, a few might even take a new mate. But they were dead, truly and for always.

"You about ready?"

"I'm scared to go back to town."

"It'll be all right."

"What if we go back and there's this crowd around the front of your office and Paul's laying there on the ground?"

"You've got quite an imagination."

"Or he's slung over the back of some horse?"

"Let's go."

"You don't give a shit, do you?"

"I didn't know you had such a mouth on you." And

instantly regretted saying it. What a stuffy, stupid, pompous thing to say to somebody in pain like hers.

He went over to her and put his hands out to her. "It's because I'm stupid. It's because I don't know the right thing to say. That's why you don't think I care about you and your brother. How about giving me another chance?"

And then she took his hands and he pulled her gently to him and let her sob as long as she wanted to against his chest.

The rain started as soon as they left the forest. They were soaked in minutes. They didn't even try to speak as they rode.

As they reached the town limits, Matthews happened to notice an odd look on Annie's face, some kind of recognition. Or was he imagining it? All that lay in front of them were the familiar buildings of the commercial area. He soon forgot about her strange expression.

The only time he looked in her direction again was when they were half a block from the sheriff's office. He saw her whole body tense up, become even more angular than usual. Body, mind, and soul preparing themselves for bad news.

But there was no bad news. Not for her.

When they walked into the office, dripping rain and numb with cold, the assistant day deputy, Devries, looked up and said, "Posse came back in. Didn't have no luck."

Relief showed clearly on Annie's face. She turned away from Matthews and the deputy for a long moment. She made a ragged sign of the cross. Thank you, Lord.

"I need to get out of these clothes," she said. "Thanks for going with me."

"I'm pouring myself some of this mighty fine coffee. You sure you don't want some?"

"No, thanks. I do a little better by coffee than you do here. Think I'll wait till I get home." She walked to the door. "You hear anything—or anything happens—you'll let me know right away, right?"

"Fast as I can."

"He hasn't had an easy life."

Matthews nodded. "I know he hasn't."

He knew what else she wanted to say. *Don't let some drunken bastard kill him. Don't get all puffed up being the law and force him to kill himself. Don't hurt him when you arrest him.* Those were the things *he'd* want to say, at any rate.

She looked at the deputy. "No sign of him at all?"

"Afraid not."

"And everybody's back in—the whole posse?"

"Yep. I counted noses personally. Everybody's in."

She'd been given a reprieve. He wasn't dead. Not yet. And maybe he wouldn't be dead. She wouldn't be foolish enough to think that he would ever be free again. But maybe he wouldn't be killed. And maybe they'd put him somewhere not quite as rough as a territorial prison. Maybe, maybe, maybe. Her little life was nothing *but* maybes now.

After she left, Devries said, "That McCabe fella was looking for you. The Pinkerton."

"He say why?"

"Just said he thought you needed to talk as soon as

possible." Devries scanned the sheriff up and down. "But first thing you better do is get out of those duds."

"Thanks, Mom."

"You'll catch your death that way. I had a cousin did just that. Got soaked in the rain and was dead by midnight."

"I didn't think pneumonia worked that fast."

Devries, an unrepentant joker, said, "Oh, it wasn't the pneumonia. My cousin's wife caught him out in the field with this gal my cousin was seeing on the sly. They were doin' it right against this limestone cliff, right in the rain. So when she got him home and in bed—he was sick and all by then—she waited till he was asleep and cut his throat."

"You and your stories," Matthews said.

"Half of 'em are true."

"Yeah, but which half?"

The deputy grinned. "Sometimes I don't even know myself."

EIGHT

THE SHORT WAY home led Annie along the north edge of town. In the rain the Presbyterian church's spire had the look of myth—a monument soaring to pierce the heart of evil itself. And when the bell rang, as it did every day, the sound filled her with an almost idiotic optimism. Yes, things would be fine. Just fine. She even told herself that she didn't need to worry. That at home she would build a warm fire, change into dry clothes, and sip hot cider. And things would be just fine.

Home seemed especially empty and drab. She built the fire, changed the clothes, drank the hot cider. But the mood wouldn't lift. She knew then that the mood wouldn't ever lift. Never. Because Paul was her brother. Because Paul would end up in prison for life or hanged.

The rain stopped. A rainbow appeared. She loved rainbows. They made her feel like an innocent child again. She went out the front door and stood in the wet grass and let the cosmic blend of rainbow colors imbue themselves upon her soul.

In the distance she saw a rider. Her assumption was that it was Paul. But the rider turned abruptly and headed toward the river. He turned into a shining black silhouette when he reached the summit of a distant hill, just before his descent into the cold gloom of the valley. The darkness always started in the valley and worked its way up.

Inside again, she lit a lamp and tried to concentrate on one of her magazines. She never got much mail. The magazines were the treat. Sometimes it took two months for them to reach here. But it was always worth the wait. Magazines inspired such dreams.

And tonight it was a magazine that inspired her to realize where her brother Paul just might be. The illustration depicted an expensive Eastern wedding, bride and groom coming down the steps of a huge church, a hansom cab waiting for them amidst a street-filling crowd in beautiful gowns and top hats.

But it was the church belfry that gripped her attention. *Paul always liked to hide in the highest place possible.* Then she remembered the Presbyterian church here, the one she'd passed in the rain earlier this evening.

Once again, an almost ridiculous sense of hope filled her, so much so that as she pulled on her boots and grabbed a dry jacket and hat, she felt light-headed.

She could picture him in the belfry. There would be perfect places to hide if it was anything like most belfries she'd seen. Even when the preacher came up the steps to ring the bell, there would be someplace for Paul to hide.

The highest place possible.

Ever since he'd been a little boy.

She gutted the fire as quickly as she could and ran out the door to saddle her horse. She would find him. And soon. She was sure of it.

Just before Annie reached the middle of town, the rain started again. It was a dismal, warm, slow rain this time. At least the earlier rain had cleansed the air. This one left a residue that made the skin feel sticky and hot.

She took her horse to an alley a block away from the church. She tied him securely to a post underneath a heavily leafed oak. She had chosen this alley because she planned to give Paul her horse. He would have a clear chance to ride straight into the foothills to the south. On a gloomy night like this, nobody would see him.

She found a side door to the church. There was no light inside. She wished there was a bank of votive candles alight, such as ones in the Catholic churches. She stood inside the imposing church, the nave lost in heavy shadow above her, the pews laid out neatly, her eyes just now adjusting to the darkness. The altar was simple but elegant. The pulpit stood three feet off the floor, on a platform mounted by three steps. The minister here was from back East. He was said to give a dandy sermon.

She walked down the center aisle. Her steps echoed

off the walls. You could smell the warm rain through a couple of half-opened stained-glass windows. She wasn't sure where the belfry steps were, just somewhere near the front of the place.

She found a door near the front doors. When she opened it, a November chill came down the vague shape of the winding stairs. The belfry. Over the years, the wood in the stairs had rotted some from rain and snow blown downward from the belfry. The edges of some steps were raw where the wood had been eaten away. The narrow walls were the same stone as the church exterior. The walls were damp and cold and reminded her of a dungeon.

She knew better than to shout out his name. She would never find him then. He'd bolt like some animal. He wouldn't be sure who she was till she was very near the top. She proceeded carefully. She wished there were more light, less wind.

As she climbed, she listened. The church had many ghostly voices—stone, wood, wind against the massive belfry bell—a living entity the church was. But the voices did not speak of her brother, did not offer a single clue.

She stepped on something bulky. Bent over to see what it was. She was able to surmise from her vague glimpse that the size and shape was that of a bird. Hard enough to be long dead. She toed it aside and continued upward.

There was a small room built into the north wall of the belfry. This was where the church kept the various tools and implements it needed to keep the bell functioning properly. This was where Paul had been hiding since just before the posse formed that first day. He'd had no food; the only water was the rain he could catch in his hands. He was stiff from cold, his sinuses raw and painful, his mind a mist of memories and fears. He had no plans. He was too confused and weak to have any plans. He knew someone would rescue him. He had no idea who. Or even why they would rescue him. But they would. They'd come along and rescue him and everything would be fine again. He wouldn't have to go back to that hospital where they'd beaten him and made fun of him and, as punishment, put him in locked rooms with truly grotesque people who filled their hands with their own feces and then rubbed it all over their naked bodies. He had decided long ago that he would never go back to that place. Never. Under any conditions.

Noise on the steps woke him completely. He'd been sitting in a corner of the small room when the sound made him jerk awake. The only other visitor he'd had was the man who rang the bell. Paul was afraid that the man would open the door and find him in here. But so far, he'd been lucky. The man had climbed the stairs, rung the bell several times, and then retreated back down the winding steps as if he was in a great hurry.

He wished it was pretty dawn again when he'd dared stand in the belfry and look out on the silver-dewed land. From here, above the human griefs inside the houses and shacks and shanties and hotels—from here the land looked like a storybook kingdom, so beautiful and tranquil with its pastures and creeks and forests.

When he was up this high, he felt safe. Nothing and no-body could harm him.

Then he heard his name spoken and his heart was filled with a great fluttering, like an ecstatic bird. He knew the voice well. The voice that had soothed and suc-cored him all his life. His sister, Annie.

With no hesitation at all, he burst from the storage room and stood at the top of the stairs where he could watch her make the last few steps of her ascent.

Annie would have ideas, good ideas. She always did.

Good, sweet Annie.

Lacking anything else to do, resisting the urge to go and see Karen Davies, Matthews decided to look up the Pinkerton, McCabe. Not in his room. Not in the restau-rant downstairs. Not in the two most popular cafés. Probably chasing somebody or something down. You rarely met a lazy Pinkerton cop. Some of them were pretty mercenary, but few of them could be accused of laziness.

Matthews ate at his favorite café. Steak and potatoes and green beans. He rolled himself a couple of cigarettes afterward. A few people drifted over to his table. They said pretty much the same thing. *Sure hope you catch Annie's brother real soon. Annie's somebody we like. But we seen her brother t'other day. There's somethin' wrong with him. You don't even have t'hear him talk. You can tell just by lookin' at him. Somethin' serious wrong there.*

He listened politely. Nodded when it was appropriate. And always looked concerned. He'd once known a sheriff who was a yawner. The fella couldn't help it. He just yawned all the time. And that isn't somethin' you appreciate when you're pouring out your heart and soul to somebody. Him yawning right through it. Last Matthews heard, the yawner was now on his sixth job as a lawman. Nice, competent fella, too. But that damned yawn of his got him in trouble in every town he went to.

Matthews listened. And didn't yawn.

At one point during his ninety-minute café stay, the cook came out with a large slice of birthday cake. Seems a family had ordered it as a surprise for their oldest son. But when they'd brought him in tonight, the flu he'd been fighting all day came up and he vomited all over the table. Now a thing like that sure ain't good for business if your business is food, the big Swede cook said. And the family run out without payin' for their meal, let alone the cake. *In a way,* the Swede said, *I was just as glad they did. Sure wouldn't want that little kid pukin' again at the height of the supper hour. So you have this slice of cake on the house, Sheriff. Our way of sayin' thanks.* What the big slice of cake was all about was the Swede's seventeen-year-old boy Roger. Kid was always getting in some kind of minor scrape. He wasn't a criminal, just a mischief-maker. The Swede obviously figured he was buying favors by giving the sheriff this amazing hunk of tasty cake.

Matthews had just put another layer of sweet cream frosting on his upper lip when Harvey Dodge came in. Harvey was another auxiliary deputy. A good one. There was a gravity about him that comforted people. Never got hysterical. Never got mean. Thought things through and did his best to keep folks from getting riled up.

Harvey sat down opposite Matthews at the small window table. Even this close, he felt compelled to lean forward and to speak in a whisper.

"We found him."

"Paul Reynolds?" Matthews asked.

Harvey was a heavy man with a wide, peasant face and coarse skin. He dropped his voice another notch. Shook his head. "The Pinkerton man. Dead."

"McCabe?"

Harvey nodded. He'd forgotten to take off his flat-crowned black hat. Matthews wasn't about to remind him.

"Shot. Twice."

"Where'd you find him?"

"Alley. Over back of the hotel where he was stayin'."

"Damn." Then: "He live long enough to say anything?"

Harvey shook his head. "Not the way I got it. They should be on their way over there now. Doc and everybody, I mean. They'll be waiting on you, I imagine."

"Thanks, Harvey."

"Sorry I had to spoil your meal."

Matthews patted his full stomach. "Everything I've had to eat tonight, I could probably survive a month before I needed to eat again."

Matthews paid off his bill and stepped outside. Full night already. No stars. Heavy gray clouds. And thunder. It was likely going to rain again.

He thought briefly about Karen. This'd be a good

night to sit in front of her fireplace and talk about days gone by.

But at the moment, Karen was less important than a dead Pinkerton in the alley behind his hotel. He could no longer worry about how Paul Reynolds could be stopped. Any way, including killing him, would have to do.

Annie held her brother the way she had held him since he was six years old. Even at that age he had imagined that people were out to harm him—even kill him; even at that age he had told her wild impossible stories of bestowing vengeance on those who mocked him or hurt him in some way; even at that age she had seen the fear that had driven him to hide from everybody, including Annie herself.

"I was so scared for you," Annie said.

Both of them spoke in whispers. Up here, in the cold and misty night, the belfry was damp as a dungeon. Rats spoke in fierce and tiny voices and ran in and out of holes where the boards of the floor met the stone of the tower. There was little room for moving around. The huge metal bell took up most of the space. It appeared to be in good shape. She could smell fresh oil on the bell bearings. The ropes appeared to be new.

"They think I killed those people, Annie. They think I killed those people and I didn't."

She almost started to say, *But you told me you did*— but you couldn't deal with Paul that way. Because his stories shifted constantly, leaving you to decide for yourself which version was true.

The Paul who'd come to her door the other day was the fairly normal Paul. The one who could act like a pretty ordinary human being as long as you didn't look too close. The one who could hold a job for a brief time, even court a girl for an evening or two. But that Paul never lasted long. That Paul invariably became this Paul—the frightened, frail man who felt persecuted by demons only he could see and hear. This was the Paul who drifted between waking nightmares and reality— this was the Paul she had always feared for. This was the Paul people laughed at and were secretly afraid of, as if he was from another world, another realm where creatures from the fog threatened to cross over into this world and destroy them.

She continued to hold him. She had never felt him tremble with such bone-cracking fury. This was verging on a seizure. His clothes were cold to the touch and his body stank of his day eluding capture. She wasn't sure but there was a vague odor that told her he had filled his pants. He got like that sometimes when the worst of the fear was on him. Couldn't even control his bowels. Just sought darkness—the ultimate hiding place—

"You told me you did, though, Paul."

"I wanted to kill 'em, Annie. After what they did to our little sister. But when I came right down to it—"

She held him away from her. Stared at him. The heavy shadows of the belfry made it impossible to see his face. "Paul, listen to me. If you didn't kill them, you need to tell the sheriff that."

"No!"

He bolted from her.

"You know what the sheriff'll do to me."

"No, he won't, he's a friend of mine."

"Friend of yours. You don't know any sheriff who's a friend of yours."

"This one is, Paul. He really is. We can trust him."

"He won't believe me."

"He will if we sit down and talk to him. Tell him how you sometimes—exaggerate things. Tell him that that's what you were doing with me. Exaggerating was all. That you didn't kill those men. Even after what they did to her."

"He'll shoot me." His trembling grew even more furious now.

She gripped him again, the way she would a drug addict in the worst stages of his unfulfilled need. "He won't. I'll be with you. I'll see that he doesn't hurt you in any way."

"You're a girl."

"I can still protect you, Paul. Haven't I protected you most of your life?"

"This is different. There's a whole posse looking for me."

"The posse doesn't matter, Paul. It's dark. They won't see us. We'll just sneak down from here and go straight over to the sheriff's office. We'll be safe there."

Paul broke away again, went over to one of the slots, and peered out at the town. He said nothing but he didn't need to. She could imagine what he was thinking, seeing the lights of the town spread out below him. How safe he felt up here. How the houses and buildings below meant people—and how people meant scorn and danger.

She wasn't sure if he was telling the truth. Maybe even he didn't know. Sometimes, he got so confused he didn't know the difference between fantasy and reality. But she suspected that he hadn't killed any of the men because he'd never actually hurt anybody before. He'd only had daydreams about it—daydreams so vivid they *seemed* real to him.

She touched his back. "You can see it from here."

"See what?"

"The sheriff's office."

"Where?"

"Down at the end of that block there—see the building on the end of the street?"

"That's it?"

"Yes."

"How come it doesn't have a star on the door or anything? Most sheriffs' offices have stars on the door or something."

She smiled. "You'd have to ask Reed, Paul."

"Reed? He's the sheriff?"

"Yes."

"And he lets you call him Reed?"

"I told you. He's a friend of mine. He's been very nice to me."

"Does he have a gun?"

"He has to have a gun, Paul. He's the sheriff."

"He'll shoot me."

"No, he won't. I promise."

"Maybe he'd come up here and talk instead of me having to go down there."

"You want him to think you're innocent, Paul. It'll

look a lot better if you go down there and see him yourself."

"You mean you won't go with me?"

"Of course I'll go with you."

"I'm just so scared they'll hurt me, Annie."

And with that he turned full toward her so she could hold him again—and then he began sobbing.

NINE

THE BODY LAY faceup, encircled by eight lanterns. Half the town, it seemed, wanted a good look at the dead Pinkerton. He looked dapper, even in death. The only sign that he might be experiencing some discomfort—gas following a too-heavy meal—was the slight frown beneath his mustache.

Death was easy enough to explain. Two shots in the general area of the heart. Loud as the gunshots had probably been, they apparently hadn't been loud enough to be heard above the tumult of the casino two doors down. A four-piece band was blasting away and had been, Matthews was told, most of the early evening. A casino girl had decided to go for a short walk on her break. She'd discovered the body. Matthews didn't sense any relationship between her and the dead man. He sent her back to the casino.

The doc came, the death wagon came, and finally the night deputy who was filling in for Harold Lincoln. Matthews walked the alley, looking for anything that might be helpful in learning the identity of the killer. Nothing. A myriad of footprints. No eyewitnesses in the few shops still open. He looked carefully for shells, too. Nothing there, either.

"Any of you ever talk to this man?" Matthews asked the crowd, unlovely frontier faces given character and appeal by the hard honesty in them, features and heavy brows flickering in the lantern light.

Nobody seemed to have spoken to him.

A woman raised her hand. "I saw him talking to Hector Nolan earlier today. Over by the newspaper."

"I seen him talkin' to you out in front of ycr office t'other day," Billy Scott said. Billy was "slow" and often said things that made people giggle. He giggled right along with them. Every once in a while, looking into his eyes, Matthews had the half-deranged idea that Billy just put on his "slow" routine so he could get away with irritating people.

"I meant *besides* me, Billy," Matthews said.

And everybody, of course, giggled as they always did.

He turned everything over to the night man and went to McCabe's hotel. No visitors that the desk clerk was aware of. No mail. No telegrams. He gave Matthews the key to McCabe's room.

Matthews got a lantern lighted in Room 208 and started looking once again for anything that might be useful in identifying the killer. McCabe had been a tidy man. Two pairs of high-backed shoes polished to a fine gloss. Clothes hung and pressed impeccably. Same for cravats and shirts.

The black leather case was the only interesting thing to Matthews. It proved to be a small vault of papers, everything neatly filed in different folders. There was one problem. The folders were named in some kind of code probably known only to McCabe, forcing Matthews to go through every single page inside the stout leather case.

He guessed that McCabe had been one of those efficient men who'd take the files of several cases along with him so he could work on them in his spare time. Reports probably needed to be written, updated, filed with the home office so that the client could be brought up to date and billed. For all the romance that surrounded his agency, Alan Pinkerton was a businessman first and a criminal-catcher second. And as far as Matthews was concerned, there wasn't anything wrong with that.

He kept looking through the pages.

Annie led him down the stairs, even holding his hand. He was slipping quickly into his ominous silence, when he shut out everything around him, including Annie's words. Sometimes, he'd just bolt and you paid hell trying to find him. Another hiding place.

The belfry steps were damp, had to be negotiated carefully. Tiny eruptions of sound, whimperings really, came from his chest and throat. She gripped his hand all the tighter. "You're going to be fine."

"They're going to kill me, Annie."

All his persecution fears were in his voice now. She was surprised that he'd even broken his silence. His words were redundant. His body language, his reluctance to go down even one more step, his whimperings told her everything she needed to know. She imagined that, if they'd been somewhere else, he would have tried to run away. But the confines of the belfry stairs made that impossible. What she was worried about was the street. When they reached it, he'd have plenty of opportunity to run away. She'd never catch him. The one sport he'd ever been good at was running. Virtually nobody could catch him. In her frantic fear she'd forgotten to check him for weapons.

Roy Fuller put his pencil down, leaned back in his desk chair, and gave himself up to the shudder that sent him into a spasm. As the accountant for the various interests of the dearly departed Vernon Davies, he frequently worked late. And he didn't mind. He'd rather be here at the office than at home pretending that his marriage was a good one. Or even an interesting one. Even their fights had been dull.

That was what the money had been going to do for him. Escape. A few years back he'd begun buying magazines and books about the South Seas. Paradise on earth. In the worst of winter, he imagined those trade winds soothing him as he leaned against a palm tree, his right hand wrapped around a cool alcoholic beverage, his left arm dangling off the warm, bronzed shoulder of a beautiful native girl who wore only the skimpiest of cloth about her loins.

Then on a trip to Denver it had started again after eight long years of abstinence, the tendency, the inclination, the *curse* that had been destroying his life since he was in his teens. They said that liquor destroyed your life, that drugs destroyed your life, that scarlet women destroyed your life. And that might all be true. But for Roy Allan Fuller, gambling was the dark seductress. It was almost funny when you thought of it. An accountant was supposed to be hawklike when it came to guarding money. Ever vigilant.

And so the money he had been stealing from fat, irritating Vernon Davies did not end up in a well-hidden metal box earmarked for the land of the trade winds and comely native girls . . . the money ended up earmarked to pay his gambling debts. His trips to Denver became more and more frequent. His debts got more and more impossible to manage. Hell, one of the casinos had even sent a thug all the way from Denver to Fuller's home to collect money. The man hadn't even tried to disguise who he was or what he wanted. He'd demanded the money right in front of Fuller's wife and children. His wife—who'd sincerely believed that he'd actually conquered his gambling habit—flung herself at the thug, saying he had no right to do this in front of the two little children. The kids, of course, began to cry. His son Roy, Jr., even hit the thug in the thigh, protecting the sanctity of his home, though at six years of age it was doubtful he thought of it in those terms.

He sat in the silence of his own sins. Sat in the silence of his own folly. Sat in the silence of his own selfishness. He wanted to believe that he was sorry because of what he'd done to his family and, he supposed, he did feel at least a bit of that. But his real remorse was for that damned trade-wind island and that endless supply of native girls. He probably would've gone about in a sarong of some sort himself. A virtual god—a white god among the stupid heathens—living out the life so many men dreamed of but not more than a handful ever achieved.

He felt buried inside it all now, especially the events of the past few days. Annie Reynolds's odd, crazed brother coming to the office and wanting to see old Vernon . . . leaving that letter for him. And Roy seeing a way out at last. He was a shrewd enough accountant to fix the books—even with the Pinkerton in town—but even better . . . what if Vernon and the Pinkerton and a couple of Vernon's friends all got themselves killed by this lunatic whose sister had been raped? Nobody would suspect that all the other people had simply been killed to cover up Vernon's murder. . . .

And if all else failed, Roy knew, thanks to Paul's drunken ramblings that night, what those four men had done to that girl. That was a powerful bit of knowledge.

He turned off the lamp. Found his way in the shadows to the front door, where he lifted his derby from the hat tree. He took his key from his pants pocket, looked around the empty office one last time, and then opened the door.

Annie and Paul Reynolds were walking down the center of the lamplit street. Well, Annie was walking. Paul was being dragged along.

It took several moments for the significance of what he was seeing to suggest a course of action. Paul

Reynolds. The troubled, possibly insane man he'd set up as the murderer. Walking down the center of the street with his sister. Nobody else around at the moment. Paul Reynolds. Wanted for murder. A dangerous man.

Old Vernon had believed in guns. Not only did he have a six-shooter in a drawer in his own desk, he insisted that Roy Fuller keep one in his desk, too.

Fuller didn't bother with the lamp. He simply dove through the gloom, stumbling, badly cracking his kneecap against the edge of the desk, swallowing up the eye-watering pain, to hell with the pain, fuck the pain— finding the second drawer of his desk. Finding the six-shooter and fitting it to his hand in an almost fond, tender fashion. But time mattered. No time for anything but bursting into the street. It was obvious where Annie was dragging her brother. The sheriff's office.

He had to kill Paul Reynolds before the man reached Reed Matthews. Killing him would mean that there would be no questions asked. Not even about the two Pinkerton men. Reynolds would be dead and the matter would be closed.

He hurried out the door, knowing enough to walk fast rather than run, so it would look like he'd come upon them by accident. He hadn't been pursuing them at all, he'd just come upon them and he saw the trouble Annie was having with him and he saw Paul reach inside his suit coat. And to protect Annie, Roy Fuller—model citizen, loyal and beloved factotum of the late and deeply grieved Vernon Davies—this mixture of fear for Annie and his anger over Vernon's death—

—well, he'd just opened fire before Paul could pull

his own gun out and kill Fuller. Now what jury was going to convict him of anything for doing *that*?

He hurried on. One last death . . .

It was done then, Reed Matthews thought. Almost done, anyway. He would need a confession to pull it all together. Vernon Davies was the center of it all; the other deaths, he was pretty sure, had been committed to cover this fact, to distract the eye. McCabe's files had told him this. The first Pinkerton man had come to town to audit Vernon Davies's books. Davies had suspected that Roy Fuller was cooking the books, hiding large amounts of embezzled money. Somehow Fuller had found out what Paul Reynolds was going to do, or, given his tentative mental state, hoped to do. . . .

He stood up, tucked the file he'd been looking through back into the leather case, and then moved quickly out of the hotel room.

The half-moon was smudged behind fat gray clouds of rain. The taste and smell of rain was on the air. He moved quickly down the street. The first place he wanted to check was Davies's office. Fuller often worked late. . . .

TEN

ROY FULLER SAW immediately that there was no
way he could shoot Paul Reynolds. As he came up
behind them in the street, Paul was resisting by throwing
what looked like a child's tantrum, shouting and waving
his arms in the air. "They're going to kill me! You don't
understand, Annie! They won't wait for a trial!"

The arms in the air—nobody would believe Fuller if
he claimed that Paul Reynolds had looked as if he were
about to grab a gun from inside his suit coat. Reynolds
was making enough noise that there were a few wit-
nesses, too, old men standing on the porch of the hotel
that served mostly drifters and derelicts. This early in the
evening, they were the only other people out and about.
The early drinkers were already in the saloons; the after-
supper drinkers hadn't ventured out yet. Except for the
six street lamps that lit the four long commercial blocks,

the light was dim. The old men probably wouldn't have paid Paul much if any attention. But he was too loud, too frantic, too scared to disregard. He was cheap entertainment in the chilling darkness that preceded the oncoming rain.

Fuller realized then that he needed to isolate Reynolds. And there was certainly a logical way to do it.

He came up behind Annie and said, "Are you having trouble, Miss Reynolds?" He'd always been pleasant to her, even though he considered her something of a slut, because old Vernon insisted that his help be pleasant to everybody. He didn't want average people spurned or belittled in his name.

"Oh, evening, Mr. Fuller. I'm afraid my brother's having some—difficulties right now."

"They're going to kill me, that's what they're going to do," Paul cried, sounding more fragile and insane by the moment.

"I'm taking him to the sheriff's office. He'll be all right once I get him there!"

"No!" Paul Reynolds shouted into Fuller's face. "No! Don't let her take me there!"

Fuller had been wondering how he was going to isolate Paul Reynolds. Well, he didn't have to. Reynolds was isolating himself.

Fuller said, "Tell you what, Miss Reynolds. Why don't you let me take him over by the river there and just sit him down for a minute on a bench? Just kind of talk to him. Calm him down. I sure hate to see somebody this scared."

"He's not well, Mr. Fuller. I'm not sure you'd know how to handle him."

"I know he's not well, but—"

"Well, I appreciate your offer but I really think I need to—"

He ran then, Paul did. Looked about as if he'd been stranded on an alien world, as if he'd never seen anything remotely like the buildings and people and moon that comprised this particular world, and set off running.

"Paul!" Annie shouted. "Paul!"

"You stay there, Miss Reynolds," Fuller shouted and set off running.

The thing was to let Paul lengthen his lead. Get just far enough ahead of Fuller to make it look as if he'd disappeared. Then Fuller could catch him. Claim that Paul had gotten so wild that Fuller had had to pull his gun. And that Paul had made a grab for it and in the process . . .

Who could blame a good citizen like Roy Fuller for trying to stop a crazed killer—without getting killed himself?

Of course, he'd drawn his gun.

Didn't he have every right to draw his gun?

Of course, he had every right to draw his gun.

He went after him, chasing the ghosts of the night, still close enough to Paul to hear the searing quality of the madman's breathing.

Annie was about to start running after Fuller and Paul, but a familiar voice stopped her. She turned to see Reed Matthews jogging up the street toward her. She saw a heavy black case in his right hand.

"Was that Roy Fuller?" he said, just before reaching her.

"Yes. And Paul. I was bringing him to your office but he got scared and took off running. Roy was nice enough to go after him."

Matthews was breathing heavily. He slammed the heavy case into her arms and said, "Hold this till I get back."

"You sound like you're mad," she said.

"I am," he said, "at myself."

Without any further explanation, he raced away, his speed doubled now that he didn't have to tow the case.

As he ran, Paul thought of two possible alternatives his life might take once they captured him. Either he would be hanged or he would go back to a hospital much like the one he'd been in. He thought of people who ate their own excrement. He thought of the man who'd strangled and raped the old woman. He thought of the guards who used to beat patients and bet on who could knock a patient unconscious first.

He ran.

Would death be better?

He stumbled once, slamming against the edge of a building. He was so frenzied with the images in his mind that he was scarcely aware of the pain for a time. But after a few minutes, not even the vivid, lurid memories of the hospital could buffer him from the raw jabs of pain that traveled the length of his arm.

He ran.

But now he was crying, sobbing.

The railroad roundhouse.

There was a section of it that was being added to. A

section deserted now that the carpenters had gone home for the day.

An ideal place to take Paul.

Roy Fuller tried to guess what the sobbing was all about. Dealing with someone as crazed as Paul, it could mean anything. But somehow Fuller identified the particular timbre of the sobs as expressing physical rather than mental pain. He wondered what could have happened to the man.

Night. And sudden rain. Slashing, slanting, merciless rain. Almost no warning. The kind of rain that sent every man, woman, child, and even most animals scurrying for cover. A cold, raw rain that would turn the dirt streets into mud holes for days, axles broken and bent, shacks washed away. But even above the drumming, dynamic rain he could hear Paul's sobs.

He had to close the distance fast or Paul would go right past the roundhouse. Chasing him across a maze of railroad tracks in rain like this would be no easy task.

It was impossible to see more than a few feet ahead. Night and the heavy rain were a shifting dark curtain.

He stumbled, righted himself, hurried on.

Paul could see the outline of the roundhouse through the rain. An open section. Stacks of new lumber. Sawhorses. This new extension had a roof but no walls as yet. A roof would at least get him out of the rain.

The rain had begun to frighten him. Sometimes rain was pretty and soft; and sometimes, as now, rain was ugly and angry, reminding him of the voices that sometimes mocked him out of nowhere, the voices the people in the hospital had told him were only in his head.

He took a kind of inventory of himself. Even this spurt of a run—not really so far when you came right down to it—had netted him a badly damaged if not broken arm; bruises and cuts and scrapes on his hands and knees and legs; and more confusion than he could tolerate.

Whom could he trust? Annie meant well, but she was willing to turn him over to the men who wanted to kill him. Sheriff Reed Matthews had a kind face sometimes, but you could never believe anything a man with a badge said. And Roy Fuller—the very first person he'd met when he'd come to town—seemed the most trustworthy of all. But you could never tell. In the hospital, there were people he thought he could trust and they all betrayed him. All told the guards everything he said and did. Just to earn favors for themselves.

He would never be dry or warm or safe again. He had never had this feeling quite so nakedly. He began sobbing in a way that threw his body side to side so violently that he felt as if he was literally flying apart.

He staggered forward into the open area of the roundhouse. Boxcars loomed all around him now. Toward the front of the roundhouse he saw light, heard mechanics talking and laughing as they worked.

A nice, dry work space. A normal life. Wife and kids. House and job. And acceptance by your fellows. Nobody laughing behind your back all the time. Nobody smirking. Sometimes he had sweet daydreams of leading such a life, of being such a man.

The sweet smell of sawdust and sawn lumber filled his nostrils. Sawn lumber smelled almost as delicately sentimental as newly mown grass. You could close your eyes and just coast on those scents, the way you could on a spring breeze.

But more important than the smells were the shapes of the stacks of lumber that would be used to finish the walls.

Perfect places to hide.

He felt he could stay here forever. Felt they'd never find him crouched behind the lumber this way. Sometimes, his feelings of gloom were so bad he pressed his hands to his head, as if he wanted to rip his head from his shoulders. But sometimes, as now, he had such a feeling of well-being, of confidence, that he wanted to shout out of pure glee. It was like being drunk, this feeling of optimism, in the very best way.

He found a neatly organized stack of lumber and slipped behind it.

Let somebody try and find him now. Lawmen or people from the hospital or people who just liked making fun of him.

Just let them try and find him now.

Roy Fuller watched as Paul Reynolds — or somebody — ducked his head from the barrage of rain and hurried into the roundhouse addition. He allowed himself a deep, satisfied breath. He had managed to put everything that troubled him out of his mind. Yes, there were loose ends to worry about; yes, things could still get troublesome even with Paul dead; and yes, the dead

Pinkertons might result in yet another Pinkerton agent being sent here.

But for now all that mattered to Fuller was killing Paul. He could never remember being this single-minded about anything in his entire single-minded life.

Killing Paul would make the world a safe and secure place—a wonderful and magical place—again.

Killing Paul. Everything would be so easy, then.

Matthews glimpsed Fuller and then lost him and then found him again. The roundhouse. A fool place for Paul to hide. A good place for Fuller to kill him because that was what he had to do if Paul was to be blamed for all the killing. Matthews had begun to wonder which of them was the craziest, Paul or Roy Fuller. A normal man sure couldn't kill all those people and still function. The guilt would hobble him. He just might go insane himself.

That was a good question, he thought. Who was crazier—Paul or Roy Fuller?

The only light inside the addition came from the far end of the roundhouse where the mechanics were working on an engine in the gleam of large industrial-sized lanterns. Their laughter was almost as loud as their tools working against the steel of the huge engine.

Fuller whispered, "Paul. Paul. I'm trying to help you, Paul. Just tell me where you are."

Fuller moved slowly between the stacks of lumber. Sawdust stuck to the bottoms of his wet shoes. He was a neat little man and this kind of sloppiness bothered him a good deal. As soon as he got the opportunity, he'd give his half-boots a good military shine.

"Paul. Paul. You know I'm a friend of yours. And you need a friend now, Paul. You need a friend more than you've ever needed one before. You need to get out of town before they find you. Because you know what they'll do if they get their hands on you, Paul. I don't have to tell you, do I, Paul? I don't have to tell you what they'll do, do I?"

Fuller cursed to himself.

Paul wasn't going to be as easy to deal with as he'd hoped. He'd thought that a simple offer of friendship, of trust, would be enough. But he hadn't thought through how scared Paul must be. Not even an offer of friendship—

A wide, healthy smile broke on Fuller's face. He didn't know what it was that Paul had nudged up against but whatever it was, it made a noise sufficient to tell him exactly where Paul was hiding.

Roy Fuller squeezed harder on the handle of his weapon and proceeded to go to the aid of his dear old friend Paul Reynolds.

The new addition to the roundhouse.

As soon as Matthews reached it, he knew that this was where the two men had gone. It made sense. It offered the largest number of hiding places without going into the yard itself. Climbing around on boxcars in a rain like this could be damned dangerous.

He wanted to shout out to Paul not to trust Fuller. Shout out that Fuller was going to kill him. Shout out that Fuller was going to blame him for all the murders.

The problem was, in shouting, Matthews would reveal his own position and he'd be exposed enough just entering the long, narrow addition. He had no doubt that Fuller would shoot him on sight and blame Paul.

An explosive moment of lightning reminded Matthews that he didn't actually have to go inside. The roof was done but not the walls. He could creep along the side until he found their hiding place. They'd be looking for him to come right straight up the middle.

He moved, gripping his Colt in one hand, holding his hat in place with the other. The wind was violent enough to make forward motion difficult.

He crouched, moving up the east side of the addition, gun ready. He walked wide enough to see that there were five stacks of lumber on this side of the addition. Assuming they were inside—and he could always be wrong—they were likely behind one of these stacks. From time to time, lightning offered him flickering glimpses of the addition's interior.

He allowed himself a moment to feel miserable. He was thoroughly soaked. His boots were like heavy, wet sponges. His clothes, despite his heavy sweating, felt not only sticky but inexplicably cold, too. His Colt had been exposed long enough that he had to worry about it, too. He hoped it was ready to fire. He sensed that he was going to need it. Fuller was at the point where he needed to—and would—do anything.

Matthews moved closer to the frame of the new section, hunching down and beginning his slow, anxious inspection of all five lumber stacks.

Nobody was behind the first one. Nor the second one.

At this point, he paused, listened. For a stray moment, he'd thought he'd heard voices. But the wind and the rain played tricks. With them at such a violent volume, it was difficult to know exactly what your ears were reporting. Noise of some kind. That was all you knew. And that wasn't a hell of a lot of help.

Now on to lumber stack number three.

He sucked in his breath. On number three, four, or five he was either going to get lucky. Or damned unlucky.

Gun drawn, he swept up on number three.

His eyes adjusted quickly to the interior of the building. Easy to see that nobody was hiding behind this particular stack.

He was just backing out into the rain to move on to stack number four when he heard the shots fired. Two of them. The noise registered first. He recognized what it was and recognized the implication—the sound of gunfire just naturally made a lawman seek cover without even consciously thinking about it—but it was too late.

He'd offered himself too easily as a target. He knew that now. But it was too late to matter. One of the bullets was already exploding away a good painful chunk of shoulder and the other was ripping into the flesh just to the left of his sternum.

He went to his knees. Some kind of pride that not even he understood made him keep from pitching over face-first. It was that same kind of pride that gave him the strength to raise his Colt and fire in the direction of the fifth stack of lumber.

That was when the strength of his odd pride gave out

and when he fell down, the right side of his face slamming against rain-besotted earth. He could feel the darkness coming, maybe the final darkness, and then his pride came back to him as he lifted his head up to see Roy Fuller coming toward him now, ready to put the final killing bullet into him.

As Fuller came closer, Matthews found that his question was answered. Who was crazier, Paul Reynolds or Roy Fuller?

Fuller was. He was making some kind of gibbering sound, half-pain, half-pleasure. Maybe all the killing— the blood frenzy it must take to relieve those people of their lives—maybe it was all too much for him to handle now.

Beneath the brim of his hat, his eyes blazed with the same sad persecuted fury you saw in Paul's eyes. Kind of funny when you thought about it. A prim, sober little man like Roy Fuller turning out to be at least as insane as Paul Reynolds.

Matthews could no longer hold his head up. He lowered it slowly to the soaked earth. He looked like a fallen soldier, the rain matting his hair against his skull—his hat lost somewhere in the downpour—one blue eye open, heavy red blood trickling from both nostrils and the left side of his mouth, washed away in the pounding rain. A warrior lost in some battle so small and insignificant that it would never be recorded anywhere except a weekly newspaper and some soon-forgotten court records.

Boots. Trousers.

Fuller stood over him now, close enough that his boots and the bottoms of his trousers were all Matthews could see. Matthews held onto his bowels and his bladder with the same pride that had kept him alive the last few minutes. The terror that others had described to him—the terror of the grave, of extinction—caused him to start making his own freakish sounds, trapped in his throat much like Fuller's own pure animal noises.

He was going to die. He tried to reckon with that, make his peace with it. But—

A bullet was fired. A single bullet.

A bullet that should have gone straight into his head.

It made a tiny flat sound as it tore into the soggy earth about a foot from Matthews's face. And then came a much louder sound and a more dramatic moment.

Roy Fuller, still clutching his six-shooter, fell down to the ground, his face about six inches from Matthews's. Fuller was already dead. There was a hole in the center of his forehead, a big ugly bloomed red flower, where the bullet had exploded outward in its exit path. Fuller's right eye was nothing more than a bloody hole.

Then, just before he finally gave in to the darkness, Matthews saw Paul Reynolds poke his crazed face down so that he could see the lawman. "I didn't have no choice but to kill him, Sheriff," he said in a dazed, childlike way. "My sister likes you so much, she woulda been real mad at me if I didn't."

Not until he woke up three hours later in a hospital bed, the bullets extracted from him, was Matthews conscious again.

ELEVEN

A PRESIDENT, A potentate, a pope could not have been treated any better than Reed Matthews was in the days of his recovery. The little hospital — soon to expand what with that aggressive young female doc pushing for it — seemed to be populated by people who had been set upon this planet for the sole purpose of keeping their sheriff comfortable, fed, clean, amused, and obeyed. While ordinary mortals had to endure the indignity of adhering to visiting hours, anybody here to see Matthews could pop in just about any time they wanted to. It wasn't as if they were here to see a human being — they were here to see the man who'd figured out who was *really* responsible for all the recent violence. And who had taken action to stop it.

Admirers brought him books, magazines, flowers, candy, liquor, even clothes that he could wear when he was back on his feet again, though he'd lost fifteen pounds and hoped to keep it off.

There were four days when Harold Lincoln was also still in the hospital. A nurse brought him down in a rattly wooden wheelchair to visit with Matthews. They laughed a lot, damned lucky to be alive and knowing it, the both of them.

Annie Reynolds came in on a sunny Sunday afternoon. She'd reduced her belongings to things that fit in two suitcases. She was taking Paul back East, to what she'd been promised via an exchange of telegrams was a clean, modern, kindly hospital for mentally troubled people. Reed told her for about the thirty-second time how grateful he was to that brother of hers, troubled or not. She gave him a quick sweet chaste kiss on the cheek and went to collect her brother. There was a train coming through in less than an hour.

Ab Soames stopped in, too. He still hadn't figured out whom he'd seen racing from his uncle's den that night, "but now that you mention it, Sheriff, it sure coulda been that Fuller feller. He sure was a snake, wasn't he?" Ab had signed on for a cattle drive. He figured two months with a bunch of cows and non-alcoholic cowhands would keep him on the straight and narrow.

The sheriff's constant companion was Karen Davies, of course. Morning, noon, night. Literally. With breaks to work on her various charitable projects. And to work on his cottage. Paint it, decorate it, furnish it. They'd decided that she would sell the estate and they'd move into his cottage. To him it had seemed an unnecessarily romantic gesture on her part. But she convinced him by asking him to spend some time thinking about living in a mansion with servants. Most folks wouldn't want a sheriff who lived so far beyond their own means, with whom they had, in effect, very little in common. If he chose life in the mansion, then he'd have to say good-bye to the badge. She was right. After some thought, he saw how that wouldn't work at all. He made a joke about taking a servant along with him when he wanted to ar-rest somebody.

There was only one problem. By his wedding day, he'd not only put back on the fifteen pounds he'd lost. He'd put on another six pounds on top of that.

He was sure happy his new bride was so beautiful. But why did she have to be such a darn good cook, too?

Spur Award-winning author
ED GORMAN

RELENTLESS

Someone is trying to blackmail Marshal Morgan
with a dirty secret about his wife—until
the blackmailer is murdered...and the
Marshal's wife is the prime suspect.

0-425-18894-9

Also Available:

VENDETTA   0-425-18364-5
GHOST TOWN   0-425-17927-3

**Available wherever books are sold or at
penguin.com**